D0861883

New Islands and Other Stories

NEW ISLANDS
and Other Stories by
María Luisa Bombal

TRANSLATED BY
RICHARD AND LUCIA
CUNNINGHAM

Cornell University Press
Ithaca, New York

First published, Cornell Paperbacks, 1988, by arrangement with
Farrar, Straus and Giroux, Inc.

*This translation has received an award from the Translation Center
at Columbia University, made possible by a grant from the
New York State Council on the Arts.*

Library of Congress Cataloging-in-Publication Data

Bombal, Maria Luisa, 1910–1980
 New islands and other stories.

 Translated from the Spanish.
 Contents: The final mist—The tree—Braids—[etc.]
 I. Title
[PQ8097.B67A23 1988] 863 88-47764
ISBN 0-8014-9538-5 (pbk. : alk. paper)

Designed by Cynthia Krupat
Printed in the United States of America

⊗ The paper in this book meets the minimum requirements of the
American National Standard for Information Sciences—Permanence of
Paper for Printed Library Materials, ANSI Z39.48-1984.

paper 10 9 8 7 6 5 4

"I am a German poet, well known on German soil;
and when they name the best names, they also men-
tion mine," Heinrich Heine once wrote in memorable
German verses. Today, in Santiago, Chile, or Buenos
Aires, in Caracas or Lima, when they name the best
names, María Luisa Bombal is never missing from the
list. This fact is even more notable when one con-
siders the brevity of her work—which does not cor-
respond to any determined "school" and which fortu-
nately is devoid of any regionalism.

I thank the stars that our paths have crossed, lo
these many years now, and I am proud to say this
publicly; as I am grateful for the opportunity of pre-
senting to the readers of that "other" America this
great friend and wonderful Chilean writer.

Jorge Luis Borges

María Luisa Bombal, the most important Latin American woman novelist of this century, was born in the Chilean resort of Viña del Mar on June 8, 1910. She received her formal education in France—attending the Ecole Notre Dame de l'Assomption and the Lycée La Bruyère before entering La Sorbonne, where she majored in philosophy and literature. Her first novella, The Final Mist, *was written in 1934 on the kitchen counter of an apartment in Buenos Aires that she shared with a then little-known poet named Pablo Neruda and his wife. An immediate success,* The Final Mist *established Madame Bombal as one of the most innovative stylists in Latin American literature. Both* The Final Mist *and her novel* The Shrouded Woman *(written in 1938) are considered masterpieces of Hispanic fiction. From 1937 to 1940 she wrote screenplays for Argentina's Sonofilm and produced most of the short stories in this volume—which are among the most anthologized stories in Latin American literature. In 1940, having journeyed to the United States as Chile's representative to the international P.E.N. conference, she met and married Count Raphaël de Saint-Phalle. She resided in this country for the next thirty years, returning to Chile*

on the death of her husband in 1970. In 1977 the Chilean Academy of Arts and Letters awarded her its annual prize for her novella The Story of María Griselda. *She died in her sleep on May 6, 1980, following a brief illness.*

Richard Cunningham

CONTENTS

The Final Mist

The previous night's storm had shaken loose the roof tiles of the old country house. When we arrived, the rain was leaking in every room.

"The roof is not strong enough for such a winter," the servants said, leading us into the drawing room; and as they were staring at me with some surprise, Daniel promptly explained: "My cousin and I were married this morning."

I was momentarily scandalized. For all that our sudden marriage had been a quiet ceremony, Daniel should nonetheless have informed his servants.

In truth, from the moment our coach had entered the domain of the hacienda, my husband had grown nervous, almost aggressive.

And that was natural.

Less than a year had elapsed since he had made the same journey with his first wife, that shy, thin girl he had adored, who was to die so unexpectedly three months later. But now, now there is something approaching suspicion in his eyes, in his look that covers me from head to toe. It is the kind of hostile expression with which you always greet a stranger.

"What is the matter?" I ask.

"I look at you," he replies, "I look at you and think that I know you too well."

He shivers. He moves to the chimney and, while

attempting to revive the weak blue flames flickering through the wet and smoky logs, goes on calmly: "Until we were eight years old, they bathed us in the same tub. Then, summer after summer, hiding on our bellies in the grass, Felipe and I spied on all the girls in the family bathing nude in the river. I do not even have to take your clothes off. I know every inch of your body, including your appendectomy scar."

So exhausted am I that instead of replying I prefer to let myself collapse on the sofa. Reclining, I watch this male body moving in front of me—this body so large and clumsy, which I, too, know by heart, which I also have seen grow and develop. For years I have been warning Daniel that if he does not hold himself straight he will end up a hunchback. And since I have frequently pulled his hair in anger, I know how strong his crispy blond curls are. Nonetheless, these restless movements, that anguished look are new to me.

As a child, Daniel had no fear of ghosts, nor was he frightened by furniture that creaked in the night. Now, since his first wife's death, he seems constantly afraid of being alone.

We go into another room, even colder than the first. We eat without exchanging a word.

"Are you bored?" my husband suddenly asks.

"I am exhausted," I say.

Leaning forward on his elbows, he gazes at me for some time, and then broaches another question: "Why did we get married?"

"For the sake of being married," I reply.

Daniel gives a brief smile. "Do you know what a great catch you have made in marrying me?"

"Yes, I know," I answer, nearly asleep.

"Would you rather have been a wrinkled old spinster who does knitting for the poor people of the hacienda?"

I shrug.

"That is the future awaiting your sisters."

I remain mute. His caustic phrases which stung so sharply less than fifteen days ago have not the slightest effect on me now.

A new and violent gust of rain hammers at the windows. I hear the incessant barking of the dogs at the end of the garden, their yelping, carried by the wind, sounding near, then far away. Daniel gets up and takes the lamp. He starts off. Following him, wrapped in an old vicuña shawl given me by the good woman who improvised and served our dinner, I realize to my surprise that his sarcasm only turns against himself. He is pale and seems to suffer.

On entering the bedroom, he sets the lamp down and turns away from me, trying to choke back a harsh sound that escapes from his throat.

I look at him amazed. A second later I realize that he is weeping.

I move away from him, trying to convince myself that the most discreet reaction is to pretend absolute ignorance of his pain. But inside, something tells me that my attitude is also the most convenient, the least involved.

More than my husband's sobbing, the idea of my own selfishness disturbs me. For I allowed him to walk into the adjoining room without so much as a gesture toward him, declining to whisper a single word of comfort. And then I undressed, got into bed, and immediately fell asleep.

Upon awakening the following morning, I find an empty furrow on Daniel's side of the bed. The servants tell me that he left for the village at dawn.

.

Only two days ago the young girl laid out in that white coffin was sitting under the vine arbor coloring postcards. And now she is imprisoned in a long wooden casket, the top of which has a built-in window so that her acquaintances may contemplate her last expression.

I approach and look, seeing for the first time the face of the dead.

A colorless face, not the slightest shadow on its wide, closed eyelids. An empty face, devoid of all feeling.

I would not dream of leaning down to call her name, because she appears never to have been alive— her dead face bringing suddenly to mind the word *silence*.

Silence, a long silence, of years, centuries, a terrifying silence invading the room, growing, filling my consciousness.

I back away hastily and make my way through the quiet mourners, bumping into several horrible wreaths of artificial flowers before I reach the door.

I cross the garden almost at a run, open the fence gate. But outside, a fine mist hangs over the landscape like a veil, and the silence is even more immense.

I descend the small hill on which the house stands alone amid cypress trees like a mausoleum; I stamp the earth, crossing the forest, trying to break the silence. But my feet merely drag in the fallen leaves, which, being wet and decomposing, do not even rustle; and all about me the stillness reigns.

I shun the silhouettes of mist-shrouded trees, so motionless and indistinct that all at once I stretch out my hand and graze the branches to convince myself they are real.

I am afraid. There is hidden danger in this static scenery, and in the frozen aspect of that dead girl up there on the hill.

The mist surrounds me. I react violently against its encroachment.

"I am alive, I exist!" I cry out. "And I am happy and beautiful! Yes. Happy! Happiness is no more than having a young, slender, and agile body."

Yet, for a long time now, I have been troubled by an obscure restlessness. One night while asleep I half glimpsed something, something that might be the cause. Once awake, I tried in vain to recall the vision. Night after night I have sought, also in vain, to recapture that dream.

A cold blast of wind whips my forehead as, without a sound, almost brushing me, a bird with reddish wings, wings the color of autumn, flashes past my

face. My fear rises anew. I break into a desperate race toward my house.

Moments later I see my husband, who slows his horse to shout that his brother Felipe, along with his wife and a friend, have stopped to pay us a short visit on their way to the city.

I enter the salon through a side door facing the bed of rhododendrons. In the shadows two figures separate, disentangling so abruptly that Regina's tousled long hair catches on the stranger's coat button. Astonished, I can only stare.

Felipe's wife fixes me with an angry expression. Her companion, a tall, dark-haired boy, bends over very calmly and unravels her long black locks, then moves his mistress's head from his chest.

Thinking of the tight braid crowning the back of my head so gracelessly, I leave them without having opened my lips.

In front of the mirror in my room I loosen my hair, my hair which is also dark. There was a time when I wore it unbound, hanging just above my shoulders. Very straight and close to my temples, it shone like silk, shaped (as I imagined then) like a warrior's helmet—which I am sure would have delighted Regina's lover. Later on, my husband made me tie up my extravagant mane, because I must try in every way to imitate his first wife—who, according to him, was a perfect woman.

It pains me to see that my hair has lost that subtle red tint that used to give off a strange glow whenever I moved my head. The color is fading; it will grow duller day by day from now on.

And before it loses its brilliance, its violence, there will be no one to tell me that I have lovely hair.

.

A two-handed chord struck on the old piano in the drawing room resounds throughout the house. There comes a brief, vibrant interval, and then a nocturne opens: hundreds of notes spinning up and down like a flight of sparrows.

I tie up my hair hastily and fly downstairs.

Regina is playing from memory. An uncertain performance, careless but full of passion.

Behind her, Felipe and my husband smoke without listening.

The music stops suddenly. Regina rises, crosses the room slowly, comes to my side, confronting me with her pale, defiant face—a paleness due not to lack of color but rather to an intensity for life, violence smoldering just beneath the surface of her smile.

Regina retraces her steps to the piano. Midway she smiles at her lover, who follows her every step with desire.

I feel as if I had fire in my veins. I go into the garden, flee through the mist to a spot near the pond where a sunray pierces my path like a lance stuck in the earth, lending to the place the golden lightness of a grotto dank with the forest's deep aroma.

A strange languishment overtakes me. I close my eyes, press myself against a tree. Oh, to throw my arms around a warm body and roll with it, bounding down an endless slope . . . In vain I shake my head to overcome this swoon-like lethargy.

Then I remove my clothes, my undergarments,

until my flesh glows with the same golden splendor afloat among the trees. And like this, naked and golden, I dive into the water.

I had no idea that I was so white and beautiful. The water elongates my body so that it takes on unreal proportions. Before now, I never dared look at my breasts. Rounded and small, they seem like tiny blossoms suspended above the surface.

I sink to my ankles in thick velvety sand. Warm currents caress and penetrate me. Like silky arms, the aquatic plants embrace my body with their long tendrils. The fresh breeze kisses the nape of my neck, cools my feverish forehead.

.

Early the following morning there is a commotion downstairs, heavy footsteps coming and going around my bed—all of which combine to reduce my dream to tatters: along with Daniel, I have been wearily opening drawers in search of a hundred objects it seems I shall never find. At last the house falls silent, awakening me.

The room is in great disorder. I see a cartridge belt left behind on the night table.

Then I remember that the men were going out hunting and will not return until late evening.

Regina rises in a bad mood. During lunch she launches into an incessant and sour harangue against the inopportune whims of our husbands. I make no comment, fearing to exasperate her more with what she calls my naïveté.

Later on, I perch on the stair steps and listen in-

tently for some sound of the men. Hour by hour I wait in vain for a distant explosion to shatter this enervating silence. It is as if the hunters had been swallowed by the fog.

How short the days are in this season. Already the west is ablaze with the setting sun. A bonfire seems to flare from every windowpane. A red flame embraces everything, and yet even its resplendence fails to diminish the mist.

Dusk, darkness, silence—unbroken by the croaking of frogs. Not even the monotonous lament of a cricket lost in the grass. Behind me, the entire house is black, dark as my despair.

I enter the drawing room, light a lamp, choking back an exclamation of surprise to find Regina asleep on the divan. Her face is smooth, the contours of her cheekbones softened, and her skin glows like polished ivory. I go to her. I never knew that a human being could be so beautiful in repose. Regina no longer looks like a woman—she seems a young girl, a very sweet and innocent girl.

I imagine her asleep like this, lying on lush carpets in a rich warm room where the floating perfume of women's hair and cigarette smoke combine to suggest some exotic, mysterious life.

Again, inside me, this pain, sharp as a scream.

I go out again to sit on the steps in the dark. Soon I see lights flickering through the trees. Silhouettes of men advance with infinite precautions, lighting their way with long, burning branches carried like torches. I can hear the panting of the hounds.

"Any luck?" I ask happily.

The only reply comes from Daniel, who grumbles: "Damned fog!"

Men and animals collapse, exhausted, at my feet. Before me, as though in offering, I see a line of poor mutilated bodies, a profusion of lifeless, mud-spattered wings.

And then Regina's lover lays a ringdove, still warm and oozing blood, in my lap.

I recoil, turning my head away with a nervous cry. Laughing at my squeamishness, the others depart, all but the young hunter, who, despite my squirming, continues to press the shameful trophy against my thighs. My indignation has almost reached the point of tears. Suddenly he tosses the bird aside, and I raise my face to his.

Intimidated by his scrutinizing gaze, I lower my eyes quickly. When next I look up, his eyes are still fixed on me. He wears his shirt unbuttoned. The odor from his chest is a mixture of hazelnuts and the sweat of a strong, clean man. I smile uneasily. Then, leaping to his feet, he goes into the house without a backward glance.

 .

The fog encroaches on the house more every day. Already it has blotted out the pine trees whose branches brush against the balustrade of the terrace. Last night I dreamed that it filtered slowly into the house through the crevices in the doors and windows—floating into my room and obliterating the color of the walls, the contours of the furniture, en-

twining itself in my hair, clinging to my body, smothering everything . . . everything . . . In the midst of this nothingness, only Regina's face was intact—with her fiery look and her lips full of secrets.

.

Some hours ago we arrived in the city, veiled by a curtain of mist hanging immobile around us, so thick that I feel its weight in the air.

Daniel's mother has ordered the servants to open the grand dining room and light all the candelabra on the long family table, where, huddled at one end, we sit shivering. But the golden wine, served in thick crystal glasses, soon warms our veins, its heat mounting quickly to the head.

Slightly tipsy, Daniel promises to restore the abandoned chapel in our hacienda. At dinner's end we have agreed that my mother-in-law will accompany us to the country.

The pain of recent days that once ached like a burn has faded to a sweet sadness that manifests itself in the form of a tired smile. I know not why I feel so weak, nor why I cannot cease smiling.

For the first time since our marriage, Daniel fluffs the pillows for me. At midnight I wake, suffocating. I twist in the sheets for a long time, unable to return to sleep. Each breath leaves me gasping for a little more air. Rising, I open the window, lean out—but the atmosphere outside is just as intolerable. The fog, obscuring all angle and dimension, muffling all sound, has transformed the city: given it the warm intimacy of a closed room.

A crazy idea overwhelms me. I shake Daniel, who half opens his eyes.

"I am suffocating. I need to walk. Will you permit me to go out?"

"Do whatever you want," he murmurs, closing his eyes.

I dress; on my way out don the straw hat that I wore when we left the hacienda. The courtyard door is less cumbersome than I imagined. I start walking up the street; cross avenues; thinking:

Tomorrow we shall return to the country. The day after, I will attend Mass in the village with my mother-in-law. Then during lunch Daniel will talk to us about the work on the hacienda. Afterwards I will visit the greenhouse, the aviary, the orchard. Before dinner I will doze beside the fireplace, or read the local newspapers. Following dinner, I will amuse myself with the fire—producing small conflagrations by carelessly stirring the coals. Very soon, the conversation will dwindle, give way to an oppressive silence, and Daniel will noisily fit the bars against the doors. Then we will go to sleep. And the next day will be the same, and so on for a year, for ten; and it will be the same until old age robs me of any right to love and desire, until my body withers and my face wrinkles and I am ashamed to show myself without artifice in the light of the sun.

I roam at random, cross unknown avenues—walking, walking, as if trying to escape. But how escape? And where? Death seems a more accessible adventure than escape. It is more than possible to wish for death because one loves life too much.

A small plaza beckons from out of the darkness and the fog. I lean exhausted against a tree, press my cheek against its moist bark. Invisible but very near, a fountain scatters a heavy shower.

Transformed into vapor by the fog, the white light of a street lamp bathes my hands in its pale beam, turning them ashen, spreading my vague silhouette on the grass. And it is then, suddenly, that I see a shadow next to mine.

A man, a young man, stands in front of me. He has light-colored eyes set in a dark face, and one of his eyebrows is slightly arched, giving to his countenance an almost supernatural aspect. From him, like an odor, comes an animal heat.

What happens next is sudden, violent, definitive. I realize that I have been waiting for him, that I must follow him regardless of where the path may lead. I throw my arms around his neck, and he kisses me without closing those luminous eyes.

And now I walk with an unknown man to guide me. He leads me to a narrow, sloping street; motions for me to stop beside a grated fence, through the bars of which I can make out an abandoned garden. After some difficulty, he unravels a rusty chain securing the gate.

The interior of the house lies in total darkness, but his warm hand searches for mine, urging me along, our footsteps resounding through empty rooms. Uncertainly, I ascend a long staircase, leaning on him instead of the banister railing. I follow, under the sway of his power, surrendering to his will. At

the end of a corridor he pushes open a door and releases my hand. I remain standing on the threshold until suddenly, from no apparent source, the room brightens—materializing into a small clean chamber with faded cretonne curtains that lend it an indefinable old charm, an air of intimacy and sadness. All the heat in the house seems to be concentrated within its walls. The night and the fog are without, waiting behind the windowpanes—striving in vain to enter, for not one atom of death can infiltrate this room.

My friend draws the curtains and, his chest against mine, presses me gently, slowly, toward the bed. So great is my longing, I feel faint; nevertheless, feminine modesty impels me to pretend fear. This elicits a smile from him—a smile that, while tender, is also ironic. I suspect that, for him, my feelings are an open book. Pretending on his part that he wishes to comfort me, he walks off, leaving me alone: sitting on the bed, staring at the floor.

After a bit I hear soft steps on the carpet, the sound I recognize as bare feet. Then he stands naked in front of me. His skin is dark, but covered with fine chestnut hair to which the light clings, so that his body seems enveloped from head to toe in filaments of light. His legs are very long, his shoulders straight, and he has narrow, boyish hips, an unlined forehead. His arms hang motionless at his sides. The grave simplicity of his attitude is like a second nakedness.

He unbinds my hair and then starts to undress me. I submit to his hands, silent but with a beating heart. I burn with the need for him to see me naked, for my lovely body at last to receive the homage it deserves.

I cry out impatiently when his fingers lose their way in the fabric.

Naked, I remain seated on the edge of the bed, he beside me—having shifted forward to contemplate my body. Under his attentive gaze, I lean back, a gesture that fills me with intimate well-being. Locking my arms behind my head, I cross and uncross my legs, each gesture bringing me intense pleasure, as if at long last my arms, my neck, my legs had a reason to exist. If this joy were the only end of love, I would consider myself already well rewarded!

He leans over me with a smile, pulling my head to his chest. I press my lips against him, rubbing my forehead, my face, on his chest, breathing in the fruit-and-vegetal odor of his flesh. I throw my arms around his waist, bury my cheek in his chest, holding him tight, all my senses alive. I hear the rise and fall of his breathing, the pounding of his heart—deep and powerful, thudding like a gong, resounding through his body as though each cell had somehow been transformed into a sonorous echo. Eager now, I tighten my embrace: wanting to enfold him, to feel the blood coursing in his veins. His strong muscles quiver under my fingers; he sighs. I hold in my arms not a physical presence but another life—with all its fragility and mystery, ebbing and flowing in my embrace. And I am trembling.

And then we roll entwined onto the center of the bed, his body covering mine like a huge hot wave that sets me afire with caresses until at last I feel him penetrating deep inside me and gathering me to him, and by then we are flowing together as on the silken

crest of an endless wave that leaves me faint with rapture, surprised to hear a sob rising in my throat, and then for the first time I moan with pleasure and experience that sweet weariness produced by the precious weight of his body resting between my thighs.

When I wake, my lover sleeps beside me: wearing a placid expression, his breath so light that I must lean over his lips to feel it. A small medal fastened to a fine, almost invisible chain adorns the soft chestnut hair on his chest—one of those ordinary little medals that children receive on the day of their First Communion. All my being grows tender at this childish detail. I straighten a rebellious lock on his temple, rise without waking him, dress silently, and leave—departing as I came: fumbling my way in darkness.

And then I am outside, opening the fence. It is not quite dawn; the trees are motionless. I run up the narrow street; cross the square, wend my way along the now familiar avenues, accompanied by a subtle perfume: the odor of my enigmatic friend. My entire body seems impregnated with his aroma. It is as if he still walked beside me, still held me in his tight embrace, or as if his blood were fused with my blood, forever.

And now here I am, lying beside another sleeping man.

"Daniel, I do not feel sorry for you, nor do I hate you; my only wish is that you never discover what has happened to me this night."

Why, in autumn, this obstinate insistence on having the avenues swept clean?

I would let the leaves pile up on the grass and on the footpaths, covering everything with their rustling red carpet until the dampness reduced them to silence. I try to convince Daniel to neglect the garden a little. I am beset with nostalgia for abandoned parks where the weeds erase every track and where uncut bushes make the paths more narrow.

The years go by. I look at myself in the mirror and see those undeniable little wrinkles under my eyes that before only appeared when I laughed. My breasts are losing their roundness, their fullness—once they were as firm as hard green fruit. My flesh sticks to my bones, and I am no longer slender, but angular—like one of Picasso's nudes. But I don't care! What matter though my body withers, if it has known love! And what matter though the years pass in a dull round of repetitive days; I once had a beautiful adventure . . . With nothing but a single memory one can endure a long and tedious existence: repeating day after day, like oxen yoked to the miller's wheel, the pedestrian gestures of everyday life.

There is someone I cannot think of without trembling. Today, tomorrow, ten years from now I may find him: here on the hacienda, waiting at the end of

a road lined with poplars; or perhaps on turning a corner in the city; or it may be that I shall never see him again. It matters not; because the world now seems full of possibilities, and I look forward to every minute, for every minute brings a new emotion.

Night after night, Daniel sleeps beside me, indifferent as a brother. But I do not complain—because for one long night (which seemed a year while it lasted) I have been held in the warm embrace of another man.

I rise, light the lamp as quietly as possible, and write:

Since that day when the aroma of your body overpowered me, I am yours. I want you. I would gladly spend my life in bed waiting for your arrival, for that moment when you press my body to your strong body as if you were its owner, as if my flesh were but another layer of your own. Even now, though far from your arms, I spend my days thinking of the moment when I threw my arms around your neck and sighed against your lips . . .

Having written this, I tear the paper into little pieces.

.

Some mornings I am filled with absurd joy. I sense that within the next twenty-four hours some huge happiness will fall my way. I pass the day in a kind of exaltation, waiting. A letter? An unexpected event? I have no idea, in truth.

I take walks, go deep into the forest, dawdle on my

return although it is late—shortening my steps to gain time, to give the day one last opportunity to produce a miracle. As I enter the drawing room, my heart is pounding.

Daniel lies on the divan, yawning among his dogs. My mother-in-law is winding a new skein of gray yarn. No one has come; nothing has happened. But the bitterness of disappointment lasts only a second. My love for "him" is so great that it rises above the pain of his absence. It is enough to know that he exists, that, albeit in some remote corner of the world, he feels and remembers . . .

.

Dinner seems to take forever. I wish only to be alone so that I may dream at ease. There is so much to think about! Yesterday afternoon, for instance, I was interrupted in the middle of a jealous scene with my lover.

I loathe being asked to join in the traditional game of cards after dinner. I prefer sitting by the fire, withdrawn from the world, searching for my lover's light-colored eyes among the red-hot coals. Abruptly they appear, shining forth like two stars, at which I stare, entranced, for hours. Never do I remember his expression so distinctly as then.

There are days when a great weariness assails me, and in vain I sift the ashes of my memory for a spark to light up his image.

He last appeared to me during a storm, materializing suddenly at my door as though borne on the fierce wind that blew down three walnut trees and

caused my mother-in-law to make the sign of the cross. His hair was windblown, ruffled, and he had the collar of his coat turned up. But I recognized him, and I swooned at his feet. And then, while I was unconscious, he took me in his arms and carried me off on that windy afternoon . . . Since that day, he has not left me.

.

Instead of autumn's usual pale offering, this warm sunny morning seems more like summer. I look for my straw hat but cannot find it. I search calmly at first; then feverishly . . . because I am afraid to find it. After a time I sigh, relieved that my efforts have been useless. There is no longer any doubt: I left it behind one night at a stranger's house. I am filled with such hope, such intense happiness that my heart feels light as a bird and I must place both hands over it to prevent it from flying away. Besides an embrace—a common bond for all lovers—something else unites us forever. Something material, concrete, indestructible: my straw hat.

.

My eyes are hollow, and frequently the house, the park, the woods spin giddily inside my brain and before my eyes.

I try to force myself to rest, but only by walking can I impress a rhythm to my dreams, bring them into the open, make them describe a perfect circle. When I am quiet they plummet earthward in crazy spirals, like birds with broken wings.

.

The day of our tenth wedding anniversary arrives. The family gathers in our hacienda—all but Felipe and Regina, whose absence is bitterly denounced.

As if to compensate for the indifference with which our marriage was viewed a decade ago, we are now showered with attention: an excessive show of embraces, of gifts as well, and a grand dinner with numerous toasts.

At the table, Daniel's cold look accidentally meets mine.

.

Today I saw my lover. I think of nothing else, announcing the joyous news over and over at the top of my voice. I need to write: today I have seen him, today I have seen him.

It happened this afternoon while I was bathing in the pond.

I usually stay there for hours, letting my body and my thoughts drift. Often I sink down, creating a gentle eddy on the surface while I glide ever lower in that mysterious world where time seems to stop, where light is solid as a phosphorescent substance, where my movements acquire a knowing and cat-like gracefulness as I carefully explore the dark windings in that cavern of silence. I find strange seashells, colorful crystals that, exposed to air, are transformed into nondescript black pebbles. I shift boulders from under which slippery creatures, roused from sleep, scuttle off into the gloom.

I was surfacing from those luminous depths when I spied, far off through the mist, a closed carriage ap-

proaching noiseless as an apparition. Swaying as they strained, the horses swerved between the trees and came clopping over the dead leaves without a sound.

Astonished, I grabbed the overhead branches of a weeping willow and, forgetting my nakedness, pulled myself halfway out of the water.

The carriage advanced slowly, halting close to the opposite bank of the pond. I watched the horses bend down and drink without creating a single ripple on the smooth surface.

My heart, my very nerves told me something of great consequence was about to occur.

At that moment I saw a man's head emerge from one of the narrow windows and turn to look down at me. I recognized on an instant the light-colored hair and dark face of my lover.

I thought to call him, but the impulse died in a kind of hoarse, unintelligible cry. I could not call him—I did not know his name. He must have seen the anguish on my face because, as if to comfort me, he smiled lightly and waved his hand vaguely in my direction. Then, leaning back, he disappeared before my eyes.

The carriage started rolling again, and by the time I had swum to the other side of the pond it had evaporated in the mist like a phantom.

I felt a light blow on my hip. Stupefied, I turned my face to find the gardener's son regarding me with equal amazement from the small raft he loves to pole around the pond.

Throwing my arms over my naked breasts, I said frantically: "Did you see him, Andrés? Did you see him?"

"Yes, señora, I saw him," the boy replied calmly.

"He smiled at me, did he not smile at me, Andrés?"

"Yes, señora. How pale you are. You may faint if you don't get out of the water soon," he said, poling away.

Pulling a net behind the raft, he went on skimming the dead leaves that autumn had strewn across the pond.

.

I live overwhelmed by happiness.

Whatever his intentions, I am certain that my friend is somewhere near.

The village, the park, the forest—all seem to be invaded by his presence. I walk far and near, convinced that he watches my every step.

I shout "I love you!" "I want you!" so that my heart's voice reaches him in his hiding place.

Yesterday a distant voice answered me, crying: "Looove!" I stopped, but after listening closely, I perceived the muffled sounds of repressed laughter. Mortified, I realized that the woodsmen were mocking me.

Yet at that very moment it seemed to me (absurd though it may be) that my friend was even nearer—as if those simple peasants had unconsciously been the spokesmen of his thoughts.

.

Docile, without desperation, I wait for his arrival. After dinner I steal away to open one of the Venetian blinds in the drawing room. Night after night, should he wish, my friend can watch me sitting by the fire or reading under the lamp. He can follow my slightest movement and become, at will, part of my intimacy. I have no secrets from him . . .

In the evenings I go out to the terrace when Andrés, returning from work, emerges from the rear of the park. When I see him in the distance with the net draped over his shoulders, his feet bare, I shudder—imagining that he brings me an important message. But every evening he turns and fades indifferently into the pine trees.

I lean back against the steps and take consolation in the thought that this drizzle patterning my face falls also on my friend's chest or perhaps slides in tiny rivulets down his windowpane.

Quite often, when everyone is sleeping, I rise up in bed and listen. The frogs suddenly stop croaking. I hear footsteps far off, coming toward me from the very heart of the night: approaching slowly, padding over the moss, stirring dead leaves, snapping the branches on the path. They are my lover's footsteps. This is the hour when he comes to me. The fence creaks. I hear the dogs' frenzied uproar; then, distinctly, a whispered command quiets them.

And all is silent once more.

But I have the certainty that my friend stands outside my window while I sleep, watching over me until dawn.

One night he sighed softly, but I did not run into his arms, because he has not yet called me.

.

I refuse to dwell on his reasons for not calling me.

Returning from town, Andrés just now informs me in his indifferent manner that one day he saw a closed carriage traveling swiftly toward the city.

The news, however, does not disturb me. My happiness rests secure in the knowledge that he will come back to me.

.

I have no idea how this could have happened—you see, Daniel had not kissed me in years.

Perhaps there was some slight intent on my part. God knows I longed for someone to alleviate my boredom in these long summer days. In any case, everything was unexpected, terrible, and my memory is blank until the moment I found myself in my husband's arms.

My body and my kisses did not set him trembling—they merely served, as in the past, to remind him of someone else. I watched his desperate performance: trying frantically to convince me that I was the sole object of his desire, but colliding time after time with the memory of his dead wife, who lay between us. After he had spent himself and collapsed on my chest, his cheek unconsciously sought the contours of someone else's breasts. He kissed my hands, my entire body—his lips searching for her still-familiar warmth, her odors and roughness. And then

he broke into tears, calling her name, shouting absurd things meant for her in my ear.

Oh, never, never did his first wife possess him more, heartbroken and hopelessly hers, than this afternoon. Poor Daniel—what began as an attempt to escape her memory has ended with the realization that she has become a part of him.

Still stretched out on the bed, I sobbed—my wet hair plastered to my temples—dying of shame and dismay. I did not move, not even to cover my nakedness. I felt without courage either to live or die. My only wish was to stave off the moment when I would have to think.

And it was to wallow in this misery that I betrayed my lover.

.

For some time now I have been unable to call up my friend's features. I fear that he has indeed abandoned me. To clear up what I am convinced is but a small misunderstanding on his part, I have composed a letter:

"My love, I have never betrayed you. It is true that all summer long Daniel and I have frequently been joined in that furious embrace born of tedium, perversity, and sadness. It is also true that we have often remained locked in our bedroom until nightfall. But I have never betrayed you. Oh, if only you would take me at my word, my sweetheart. By obliging me, like some silly lover, to define and explain, you turn a brief summer caprice into rank infidelity.

"Shall I go on? Very well.

"My second intimacy with Daniel took place on one of those sweltering afternoons when the house was like a fiery cage that held us trapped face to face, almost crying from enervation and boredom. The act itself was but a repetition of our first disheartening encounter: the same desperate ardor on Daniel's part, his same tearful invocation of my predecessor, and the same mutual disillusion. In the aftermath, as before, I lay inert—humiliated and yet sensually gratified.

"And then a miracle happened.

"A soft breeze feathered across my face, wafting a delicate, clear river odor that filtered through the room to the accompanying murmur of the first summer rain.

"Inexplicably, I felt less sad. Then a hand brushed my shoulder, and I turned to find Daniel standing by the bed: a friendly smile playing on his face as he extended an icy crystal glass beaded with transparent pearls, frosty vapor seeping over the brim like smoke.

"I was making a halfhearted attempt to raise my head when, with unusual tenderness, he cradled an arm around my neck and held the glass, containing ice-cold strawberry nectar, to my dry lips.

"A warm sense of well-being invaded me.

"Outside, the song of the rain rose an octave, the melody swelling in tempo as the shower multiplied itself strand by silver strand. The window curtains billowed in the soft breeze.

"Daniel came back to bed and we lay side by side for hours without a word until finally the rain began to dissipate, fading slowly, ever so slowly, out of sight and sound like a distant flight of waterfowl.

"By then the bedroom was submerged in a blue twilight in which the mirrors, shining like miniature lagoons, resembled those small pools of clear water reflecting sunlight in the Andes.

"When my husband lit the lamp, a tiny spider on the ceiling, surprised in who knows what twilight dreams, scurried off to hide. 'A good omen,' I whispered, closing my eyes again. I had not felt such a divine and simple happiness for months.

"And now, do you see why I took up with Daniel once more?

"His embrace meant nothing to me, little more than a ritual—predictable as the postcoital drink he never failed to serve me, and after this we would rest together for a long time on the wide bed.

"With the light-colored silk curtains drawn, the room by daylight was like a great pink tent full of shadowy corners and rosy light, where hours passed without anguish or irritation, where at times, enclosed in its hazy, womb-like warmth, I could imagine a heat-dazed army marching on dusty roads, or soldiers deploying across a burning plain—so hot it cracked the soles of their boots. Or I would call up cities boiling under an implacable summer sky: cities of empty streets and shuttered stores, soul-less cities, skeletons made of tar, melting in the sun.

"Thus would my mind wander, the room growing

close as a cocoon and my throat constricting as though a knot were being drawn tight around my neck, until the heat dissolved, as always, in the afternoon rain. And as the day cooled I felt that same sense of well-being sweeping over me like the breeze fanning the room with its moist breath, caressing my feverish temples like a wet cloth.

"Oh, my beloved friend—can you now understand that I have never betrayed you?

"It was all a caprice, a harmless summer caprice. You are my first and only love."

.

Today they set fire to every pile of dry leaves in the garden, which was soon blanketed in smoke that hung heavy in the air like fog. Tonight I cannot sleep. I toss and turn, leap from bed to open the window, only to find the silence without as overwhelming as the stillness in our closed bedroom. I lie down again, falling at last into a dream.

There is a head resting on my chest, Daniel's head, growing heavier by the minute—an oppressive, suffocating weight. I awaken suddenly, remembering that I first met him on just such a night as this . . . Perhaps the moment for our second encounter is at hand.

I toss a coat over my shoulders. My husband stirs. Half asleep, he mumbles: "Where are you going?"

"For a walk. I am suffocating in here . . . Don't look at me like that—I've gone out by myself this late before."

"You have? When?"

"One night when we were in the city."

"Don't talk nonsense. You must have dreamed it. I don't recall your ever going out alone at such an hour."

Trembling, I clutch his arm.

"No need to shake me—I am wide awake."

Fighting to keep my voice calm, I say: "You remember: it was a misty night. We ate in the big dining room, by candlelight . . ."

". . . Yes, and drank so much wine that we both slept like the dead."

"No!" I shout. "I beg you: remember, please remember!"

Daniel stares at me for a second, then asks spitefully: "And did you meet any people on your nocturnal outing?"

To annoy him, I answer truthfully: "A man."

"And did he speak to you?"

"Yes."

"Describe his voice."

His voice? What *was* his voice like? I do not remember. But how can that be? I can feel myself turning pale. I cannot recall his voice, because . . . I have never heard it. The events of that extraordinary night flash by in succession before my eyes, leaving me limp with the realization that my friend has never spoken a single word to me.

Daniel analyzes my expression, then says: "So. He didn't speak to you. Oh, well—he was probably just a ghost."

·

Doubt gnaws at me—an absurd but unsettling mistrust of my own mind that rankles like an ulcer in the chest. For Daniel is right: that night in the city I drank a great deal without realizing it, I who never drink . . . But that unfamiliar plaza where I first saw him—does it exist only in my dreams? And what of my straw hat? Where did I lose it, then? My God! Is it possible for a lover not to utter one word throughout an entire night? Daniel is right: only in dreams do people move so silent and ghost-like.

.

Andrés! Why did I not think of him sooner?

I will seek him out and ask: "Andrés, you are not the sort who sees visions, are you?" "Oh, no, señora. Never." "Do you remember that stranger in the carriage?" "As though it were yesterday. And I remember that he smiled at the señora."

I'll not press him further. No need—he will have said enough to save me from this terrible uncertainty. Because if someone else can testify to the existence of my lover, I shall assume that Daniel has simply forgotten my leave-taking on the evening in question.

"Where is Andrés?" I ask his parents, who sit outside their cottage.

"He left early this morning to clean the pond," they say.

My voice is nervous, loud: "I didn't see him there on my way here. And I need to talk to him soon, right away!"

They call his name, go off to look for him in the garden, the park, the forest. Then I am told: "Maybe

he went to town without telling us. The señora should not excite herself. He will show up shortly, the lazybones."

I waited all day, but Andrés did not appear. The following morning they found his canvas jacket on a raft floating near the edge of the pond.

"The net," Daniel explained. "It must have snagged on something and he was dragged under. Poor kid, he didn't know how to swim and—"

"What are you saying," I break in, shaking him, shouting like a madwoman. "No! He has to be alive! You must keep looking for him!"

Two days later they dredge his livid corpse from the pond. Standing beside his father, who sank to his knees in silent grief as they brought Andrés ashore, I went over to his body, touched him, called his name—staring at his empty eye sockets and those ruined, putrid lips that death had rendered silent and water and time had all but effaced.

And now, how will I go on?

.

Night after night I hear the far-off rumble of passing trains. And I watch the dawn creep slowly into our bedroom, ushering in another day with a sad and dirty light. On Sunday the village bells clang every hour to announce Mass, beginning with the early service at six o'clock—the hour at which my mother-in-law and two old-maid servants rush off to pray. And each morning I listen to Daniel's rhythmic breathing give way to a labored awakening. Then he sits up in bed and I close my eyes, feigning sleep.

I do not cry during the day, but suffer from chills that set me shivering from head to toe without respite, so that my hands shake like an old woman's with palsy.

Oh, to be struck down by some real illness! How I long for a high fever, or to be racked with pain sharp enough to take my mind off this doubt.

.

And I said to myself: If I could forget, forget everything—my adventure, my love, my torment; if I could resign myself to live as I did before that fateful trip to the city, perhaps then I could regain my peace of mind . . .

So I began forcing myself to slow down, concentrating my imagination on the basic necessities of life, keeping myself occupied every minute of the day.

For example, I devoted an entire afternoon to the observation of our gardener salvaging large clumps of climbing plants that the wind had blown down. On another occasion I had every ceiling in the hacienda swept clean of spiderwebs. Odd jobs became an obsession: I mended sweaters, even summoned the village locksmith to open an old glass-faced cabinet full of long-neglected books that needed dusting.

I sought to keep my dreams at bay by trying to recapture simple pleasures, such as choosing a horse and joining our foreman on his daily ride around the fields, or picking mushrooms with my mother-in-law, or merely learning how to smoke.

And it was all sheer folly.

For he was always there, lurking behind every door, inescapable, impossible to forget—stamped indelibly on my life like an image on porcelain. Everything around me was saturated with my feelings; at every turning I stumbled against a memory. The forest, because there I wandered for so long with my melancholy and my illusion; the pond, because standing on its banks one day I saw my friend while bathing; the flames in the fireplace, for in their flickering light his face appeared to me every night.

Inescapable also was the pain of remembrance, the wounding power of things—objects that pricked my mind like darts tipped with poison for which there was no antidote.

And I could not look at myself in the mirror, because my body reminded me of his caresses.

My very gestures served to resurrect him—as when, unable to break my old habit, I would stretch out my arms to embrace an invisible partner, only to feel his strong shoulders once again. It was only on those nights when I rose half-asleep to write that I would suddenly remember, staring at the pen in my hand, that my lover was dead.

I ask myself how long it will be before I am released from this fixation, before I cease to be troubled by reflections from the past. I clutch at straws—a few minutes of peace, enough to give me hope that at last I have been reprieved. But no sooner does hope surface than some remembrance begins squeezing my heart, and then comes the pain, no matter how hard I resist, biting deep with bitter teeth, sawing at my

breast, while I scream with my mouth shut so that no one will hear. Because I am sick and ashamed of my sickness.

And I cannot forget.

And even if I could forget, how would I go on living?

For well do I know that people and things and the days of my life are rendered bearable only by this state of mind created by my passion.

My lover is more to me than love—he is my reason for being, my yesterday, my today, my tomorrow.

.

The news reaches us early one morning in the form of a telegram that my husband, extremely agitated, waves at me like a fan. While I am shaking the sleep from my head, Daniel bounds out of the room to pound rudely on his mother's bedroom door. The message is succinct: Regina is at the point of death. No explanation. We must leave for the city without delay.

I sit up in bed, filled with a sudden, almost savage happiness. To go to the city and there find the surcease for all my anguish. To walk those same streets, search for that mysterious house, see the stranger, talk to him, and maybe . . . maybe . . . but I must rein in this dream lest it run away with me. Already my joy is fierce enough to send me springing out of bed.

Only then do I remember that the source of my high spirits is another's tragedy. Subdued by this

somber fact, I collect our luggage, giving orders to the maids in a grave voice.

On the train I ask the cause of Regina's illness. Daniel and his mother stare at me in amazement, their faces pinched, indignant: "Why are you always so absentminded? Can't you see that we are all upset precisely *because* the telegram was so vague? It is quite possible that Felipe did not wish to alarm us unduly. It may well be that Regina is already . . . I *swear*, your distraction borders on madness . . ."

I make no reply. During the rest of the trip, aglow with expectation, it is all I can do to keep from smiling.

.

We form a sinister group in the clinic waiting room, Daniel, his mother, and I—standing close together, morose, silent, staring suspiciously at a wide green door beside the receptionist's cubicle. It is a cold and misty morning. Our legs are numb from the long walk; numb, too, our hearts with anguish.

Were it not for the smell of ether and disinfectant, I could imagine myself back in the parlor of the convent where I was educated. The same impersonal, detestable furniture; the same tall windows, naked and narrow, overlooking a muddy park much like the one I so hated in those days.

The door opens. Felipe emerges. He is not pale, his suit is not rumpled, his hair not unkempt, and his eyes show no sign of prolonged weeping. He wears a tragic expression, speaks in a cold, dark voice. "She shot herself. They aren't sure she will live."

His mother groans, then throws her arms around his neck, sobbing. "My poor Felipe!"

Felipe embraces her, bringing his arms up and around in a slow, automatic gesture, calm as a sleep-walker, almost as if he were comforting her . . . Daniel rubs his forehead, hooding his eyes.

In a low voice Felipe tells me: "They found her in her lover's house." Hence his neat attire, the unshed tears.

I look at what he has become, feeling contempt for his petty wounded pride, this wearing of decorum as though it were a suit of armor. I know that I should pity him, but I don't. Instead, I go to a window, press my forehead against the mist-darkened panes. Like Felipe's, my heart is frozen hard when it should have long since melted.

Regina. Weeks of inward struggle, of desperate and confusing gestures: signals for help, like those of a drowning woman thrashing in the waves; long nights spent on the edge of madness; coming up from sleep's temporary solace into the clear cruel light of day—the nightmare of time and circumstance driving her to the cliff, to this final act.

Regina knew that burning pain which cannot be supported, a pain that will not be waited out, that lasts and lasts until suddenly one can no longer face it another day.

I understand her and yet I am unmoved. Selfish! Egoist! I reproach myself. But in reality I feel no guilt over my lack of compassion. Am I not, after all, more miserable than Regina?

She at least experienced the intense and complex emotions of a life full of passion; whereas I have but a single memory to sustain me, a memory whose fire must be fed daily with the fuel of imagination lest it go out, a memory so vague and remote that it almost seems a fiction. Regina's undoing was a consequence of love, true love—made up of years, of letters exchanged and secret caresses, of arguments and blows and reconciliations, of tears and trysting places. I am but a casualty of my own invention, suffering from self-inflicted wounds. Compared to Regina's, my life has been a charade performed in shadows; and I know now, truly, that I am utterly, irrevocably lost.

And now at last come the tears, brought on by pity not for Regina but for myself—my grief exploding in short monotonous sobs, ridiculous as hiccups, producing consternation in the waiting room.

They lay me on a sofa, force a bitter liquid down my throat. Someone pats me on the shoulder in a fatherly, exasperating manner while a serious-looking gentleman, a perfect stranger, speaks to me in that low and reassuring voice doctors usually reserve for the seriously ill.

But I pay no attention to him, having already decided what I must do.

.

My temples are feverish, my throat dry, and I am surrounded by a viscous spectral fog in which my very limbs seem to float like disembodied objects. The muffled sound of my footsteps, which at first gave me confidence, now unnerves me. An eerie moon glides

in and out of dark, distorted clouds. I have the sinking feeling that someone is stalking me, bent on no good.

I myself am in pursuit of a house with shuttered Venetian blinds, enclosed by a rusty fence. But this cursed fog! For two hours I have wandered, praying for a wind to lift this gray and murky veil, trying to find those two dry and twisted trees that frame the façade, seeking that narrow sloping street where moss grows between the flat, uneven paving stones.

But I keep going in circles, cannot even find the starting point: that small plaza where the stranger took my hand—although I am positive that my route is an exact duplicate of the one I followed on that faraway evening. I feel isolated, cut off from the city and all it contains by this smoky barrier, become a blurry figure upon an indistinct landscape, moving with quickening strides along empty, ominous streets.

And the silence!—so all-embracing that my footsteps seem intolerably loud, seem the only noise in the world: ringing out as they rise into the night, sound waves on a cosmic journey, transmitting their mysterious message, this resonant staccato, to whoever listens among the stars.

Then all at once, the vapor parting, a bench materializes before me. Exhausted, the fever now racing through my entire body, I collapse on the cold stone seat.

Moments later, a breeze of unusual freshness blows its breath upon the nape of my neck, brushing my shoulders with a cool caress. I turn, glimpse trees

wavering in the fog. I am sitting on the edge of a plaza whose fountain has fallen silent but whose green paths exhale an odorous humidity.

I get up without a word and start running: take the first street on my right, turn at the corner and perceive, towering between those two trees with thick gnarled branches, the dark patina of a familiar façade.

My lover's house, the Venetian blinds still shut. What a pleasure to savor the knowledge that I am in front of his house, enjoying the view of the abandoned garden. I press against the fence to certify the solidity of those cold iron bars. It was not, it was not a dream!

I shake the fence in my excitement, whereupon it opens with a creaking warble. I step cautiously into the yard, then run up the front steps and press the doorbell, setting off a distant echoing ring within. Several minutes go by. I am about to leave when the door opens. A sudden vertigo engulfs me.

An elderly manservant invites me inside with, instead of words, a retiring bow and a sweep of his arm. I find myself in a hall adjacent to a large corridor of windows looking onto a flowery, well-lighted patio.

"I will notify the señora," the old man suggests, going off.

The señora? What señora? And what does this house have to do with my dreams? The furniture is in poor taste; the curtains and wall coverings are both ill-matched and garish; and in one corner hangs a cage wherein two canaries perch. On the walls,

portraits of conventional people—not one of which bears any likeness to my stranger.

A distant moan ruptures the silence: a quiet, drawn-out cry of lamentation that seems to come from the second floor. An unexpected sweetness fills me. To find my bearings, I close my eyes as on that long-ago night of love, groping my way up a rug-covered staircase and stumbling along a series of narrow corridors, the moaning sound grown keen now and coming closer with each step. I come to a final door, push it open, look.

What has become of the smooth large bed? And where are the melancholy old cretonne curtains? The walls are covered with books and maps. Under a tall lamp, a young boy faces a music stand, practicing the violin.

The old servant waits respectfully at the bottom of the stairs.

"The señora is not at home," he intones.

"And her husband?" I ask.

His cold voice answers: "The señor? He passed away more than fifteen years ago." My look of disbelief prompts him to continue calmly: "He was blind . . . slipped on the stairs . . . we found him dead . . ."

I bolt past him, flee.

.

I wandered for a time through the ghost-like city, crossing and recrossing avenues in the hope that I had mistaken the house. But at last, unable to distinguish anything through the fog, I gave up the search, aban-

doning all further struggle against my fate. The house and my love and my adventure—all had disintegrated in the dark swirling vapor that now blotted out the moon. I was light-headed with fever, which by then had seized my throat like a burning claw.

.

Once again, this singular hospital smell. Daniel and I walk from ward to ward, going past cave-dark rooms where shadowy figures sigh, tossing and turning.

They say she has lost a lot of blood, I think to myself as a nurse shows us into a room where a woman lies face up on a white wrought-iron cot.

Regina looks so ugly that she seems another person. They have cut her hair. The once long and luxuriant locks are straight and stringy: hanging gracelessly halfway down her neck, bathed in sweat. Her nostrils are pale, so thin they seem almost transparent, and one of her hands, twitching weakly, rests on the sheet. Her eyes are half closed, her breathing labored.

I lean over, stroke her emaciated hand, regretting it immediately as, at my touch, she stiffens as if the contact of our hands had produced a violent electric shock: her head rolling from side to side on the pillow, a strangled cry of pain exploding from her parched lips in one long, wavering note; next, sitting up abruptly, only to fall back heavily on the bed and burst into tears, her cry now low and throaty as she calls for her lover: tenderly at first but then suddenly screaming threats and insults at him before her voice breaks, dropping to a choked whisper—in her delir-

ium begging for death and in the next breath praying
that her life be spared so that she might see her lover
again, but pleading with the nurse to deny him en-
trance to her room while she still reeks of ether and
blood. Then she breaks down in tears.

I hear voices murmuring that Regina has been like
this, suspended in a state of constant exaltation, since
she came out of the anesthesia . . .

My heart lurches, pounding hard. I have a vision of
Regina collapsing on a wide, still-warm bed. I imagine
her clinging to a man, fearing to fall into the abyss
that is opening beneath her—into which later she
would so arrogantly decide to fling herself. As they
carried her to the ambulance, face up on the stretcher,
she must have seen a myriad of tremulous stars defy-
ing darkness in that vast autumn sky. I conjure up a
momentary picture of her terrified lover holding in
his trembling fingers two blood-spattered braids sev-
ered with one sharp coupling of scissors.

And suddenly I feel hatred for Regina; feel envi-
ous of her suffering, her tragic love affair, envying
even the possibility of her death. There comes over
me a furious desire to grab her and shake her till her
teeth rattle, demanding to know what she has to com-
plain about, she who has had everything!—love, the
dizzying violence of passion, and the great deliverance
that comes like a calm when the storm of sex has
passed.

An ambulance comes wailing up the hospital drive
at the exact instant that we are leaving. I step back
against the wall to let it pass as several attendants

under the awning by the entrance give the bleak, professional facts: ". . . A young fellow . . . run over by a car . . ."

The act of throwing oneself under the wheels of a vehicle requires a kind of unconsciousness. I will close my eyes and try not to think.

.

Two hands grip me brutally, jerk me back just as a hot, deafening blast of wind roars past my face. I stagger, lean against the chest of the imprudent gentleman who believes that he has saved my life.

Dazed, I raise my head, see a dim stranger with a red and withered face. I tear myself from his grasp, realizing that the features are my husband's. For years I have looked at Daniel without seeing him. How aged he suddenly seems! Is it possible that I am the companion of this old man? Then I remember that we were the same age on our wedding day.

And like a blow comes the vision of my naked body lying on a slab in the morgue: wizened flesh sticking bone-tight to a rigid skeleton, between the hips a dried and sunken womb . . . What more repugnant and useless gesture than the suicide of a woman approaching old age! Is not my life already at the stage where the beginning of death is clearly marked? As for dying in order to escape—escape what new disappointments? What further suffering? Some years ago, perhaps, it might have been reasonable to destroy in one rebellious impulse all the vitality accumulated inside me to avoid watching it languish and die for want of an outlet. But an implacable

destiny has stripped me of even the right to search for death, has instead led me slowly and cruelly to an old age devoid of passion, of memories . . . of a past.

Daniel takes my arm and starts walking as if nothing had happened. He seems unconcerned about the incident. I recall our wedding night . . . Now, in turn, he pretends complete ignorance of my suffering. Perhaps that is best, I think, following him.

Following him toward an infinity of insignificant tasks; toward a thousand trifling amusements; following him to live correctly—to cry from habit and smile out of duty; following him to die, one day, correctly.

Around us the fog settles over everything like a shroud.

The Tree

To Nina Anguita:
great artist, magical friend,
who gave life and breath to my imaginary tree,
I dedicate this story which, unknowingly,
I wrote for her long before we ever met

The pianist sits down, coughs from force of habit, and concentrates for a moment. The clusters of lights illuminating the hall gradually dim until they glow like dying embers, whereupon a musical phrase rises in the silence, swells: clear, sharp, and judiciously capricious.

Mozart, maybe, Brígida thinks to herself. As usual, she has forgotten to ask for the program. Mozart— or perhaps Scarlatti . . . She knew so little about music! And it was not because she lacked an ear or the inclination. On the contrary, as a child it had been she who demanded piano lessons; no one needed to impose them on her, as was the case with her sisters. Today, however, her sisters could sight-read perfectly, while she . . . she had abandoned her studies after the first year. The reason for the inconstancy was as simple as it was shameful: she had never been able, never, to learn the key of F. "I don't understand—my memory serves me only to the key of C." And her father's indignation! "Would that I could lay down this burden: a miserable widower with children to educate! My poor Carmen! How she would have suffered with such a daughter! The creature is retarded!"

Brígida was the youngest of six girls—all endowed with different temperaments. She received little at-

tention from her father, for dealing with the other five daughters reduced him to such a perplexed and worn-out state that he preferred to ease his burden by insisting on her feeblemindedness. "I won't struggle any longer—it is useless. Leave her alone. If she chooses not to study, so be it. If she would rather spend her time in the kitchen listening to ghost stories, that is fine with me. If she favors playing with dolls at the age of sixteen, let her play." And so Brígida had kept to her dolls, remaining almost totally ignorant as far as formal education was concerned.

How pleasant it is to be ignorant! Not to know exactly who Mozart was—to ignore his origins, his influences, the particularities of his technique! To simply let oneself be led by the hand, as now . . .

For in truth Mozart leads her—transporting her onto a bridge suspended above crystal water running over a bed of pink sand. She is dressed in white, tilting on one shoulder an open parasol of Chantilly lace, elaborate and fine as a spider's web.

"You look younger every day, Brígida. Yesterday I ran into your husband—I mean, your ex-husband. His hair is now completely white."

But she makes no reply, unwilling to tarry while crossing the bridge Mozart has fabricated toward the garden of her youth.

Tall blossoming spouts in which the water sings. Her eighteen years; her chestnut braids that, unbound, cascaded to her waist; her golden complexion; her dark eyes so wide and questioning. A small mouth with full lips; a sweet smile; and the lightest, most

gracious body in the world. Of what was she think-
ing, seated by the fountain's edge? Of nothing. "She
is as silly as she is pretty," they used to say. But she
did not mind being silly, nor acting the dunce at
parties. One by one, her sisters received proposals of
marriage. No one asked her.

Mozart! Now he conducts her to a blue marble
staircase on which she descends between two rows of
ice lilies. And now he opens a wrought-iron gate of
spikes with golden tips so that she may throw herself
on Luis, her father's intimate friend. From childhood,
she would run to Luis when everyone else abandoned
her. He would pick her up and she would encircle
his neck between giggles that were like tiny bird cries
and kisses she flung like disorderly raindrops on his
eyes, his forehead, and his hair—which even then
was graying (had he never been young?). "You are a
necklace," Luis would say. "You are like a necklace
of sparrows."

For which she had married him. Because at the
side of that solemn and taciturn man she felt less
culpable for being what she was: foolish, playful, and
indolent. Yes—now, after so many years, she real-
izes that she had not married Luis for love; yet she
cannot put her finger on why, why she left him so
suddenly one day . . .

But at this moment Mozart takes her nervously by
the hand, drawing her into a rhythm second by sec-
ond more urgent—compelling her to retrace her steps
across the garden and onto the bridge at a pace that
is almost like fleeing. And after stripping her of the

parasol and the transparent crinoline, he closes the
door on her past with a note at once firm and sweet—
leaving her in the concert hall, dressed in black,
applauding mechanically as the artificial lights re-
kindle their flame.

.

Again shadows, and the prelude of silence.

And now Beethoven begins to stir the luke-
warm tide of his notes beneath a vernal moon. How
far the sea has retreated! Brígida walks seaward down
the beach toward the distant, bright, smooth water;
but all at once the sea rises, flowing placidly to meet
and envelop her—the gentle waves pushing at her
back until they press her cheek against the body of a
man. And then the waves recede, leaving her stranded
on Luis's chest.

"You have no heart, you have no heart," she used
to say to him. His heartbeat was so faint that she
could not hear it except in rare and unexpected mo-
ments. "You are never with me when you are by my
side," she would protest in their bedroom when, be-
fore going to sleep, he would ritually open the eve-
ning paper. "Why did you marry me?"

"Because you have the eyes of a startled fawn," he
would reply, giving her a kiss. And she, abruptly
cheerful, would proudly accept the weight of his gray
head on her shoulder. Oh, that silvery, radiant hair!

"Luis, you have never told me exactly what color
your hair was when you were a boy. Or how your
mother felt when you began going gray at the age of
fifteen. What did she say? Did she laugh? Cry? And

you—were you proud or ashamed? And at school—
what did your classmates say? Tell me, Luis, tell
me . . ."

"Tomorrow. I am sleepy, Brígida. Very tired. Turn
off the light."

Unconsciously, he would turn away from her in
sleep; just as she unconsciously sought her husband's
shoulder all night long, searching for his breath, grop-
ing blindly for protection as an enclosed and thirsty
plant bends its tendrils toward warmth and moisture.

In the mornings, when the maid would open the
Venetian blinds, Luis was no longer next to her. He
had departed quietly without so much as a salutation,
for fear the necklace of sparrows would fasten ob-
stinately around his neck. "Five minutes, five min-
utes, no more. Your office will not disappear if you are
five minutes late, Luis."

Her awakenings. Ah, how sad her awakenings!
But—it was curious—no sooner had she entered her
boudoir than the sadness vanished as if by an en-
chantment.

Waves crash, clashing far away, murmuring like a
sea of leaves. Beethoven? No.

It is the tree outside her dressing-room window.
She had only to enter the room to experience an al-
most overpowering sense of well-being. How hot the
bedroom always was of a morning! And what harsh
light! By contrast, in the boudoir, even her eyes felt
rested, refreshed. The faded cretonne curtains; the
tree casting shadows that undulated on the walls like
cold, moving water; the mirrors refracting foliage,

creating the illusion of a green and infinite forest. How enjoyable that room was! It seemed a world submerged in an aquarium. And how that huge rubber tree chattered! All the birds in the neighborhood took refuge in it. It was the only tree on that narrow, falling street that sloped from one side of the city directly to the river.

"I am busy. I can't be with you . . . Lots of work to do, I won't be home for lunch . . . Hello—yes, I am at the club. An engagement. Eat and go to bed . . . No. I don't know. Better not wait for me, Brígida."

"If only I had friends!" she would sigh. But she bored everyone. "If I tried to be a little less foolish! Yet how does one recover so much lost ground at a single stroke? To be intelligent, you must start very young—isn't that true?"

Her sisters' husbands took them everywhere, but Luis—why had she denied it to herself?—had been ashamed of her, of her ignorance, her shyness, even of her eighteen years. Had he not urged her to pretend that she was at least twenty-one, as though her youth were an embarrassing secret they alone shared?

And at night—he always came to bed so weary! Never paying full attention to what she said. He smiled, yes—a mechanical smile. His caresses were plentiful, but bestowed absentmindedly. Why *had* he married her? To continue their acquaintance, perhaps simply to put the crowning touch on his old friendship with her father.

Maybe life for men was based on a series of established and continuous customs. Rupturing this chain

would probably produce disorder, chaos. And after, men would stumble through the streets of the city, roosting on park benches, growing shabbier and more unshaven with each passing day. Luis's life, therefore, was patterned on keeping occupied every minute of the day. Why had she failed to see this sooner? Her father had been right: she *was* retarded.

"I would like to see snow sometime, Luis."

"This summer I will take you to Europe, and since it will be winter there, you shall have your snow."

"I am quite aware that winter in Europe coincides with our summer. I am not *that* stupid!"

At times, to rouse him to the rapture of true love, she would throw herself on him and cover him with kisses: weeping, calling: "Luis, Luis, Luis . . ."

"What? What is the matter? What do you want?"

"Nothing."

"Why do you cry out my name like that, then?"

"No reason. To say your name. I like to say your name."

And he would smile benevolently, pleased with the new game.

Summer came—her first summer as a married woman. Several new business ventures forced Luis to postpone the promised European trip.

"Brígida, the heat will be terrible in Buenos Aires shortly. Why don't you spend the summer on your father's ranch?"

"Alone?"

"I would visit you every week, from Saturday to Monday."

She sat down on the bed, primed to insult him. But she could not find the hurting words. She knew nothing, nothing—not even how to offend.

"What is wrong with you? What are you thinking of, Brígida?"

He was leaning over her, worried, for the first time in their marriage unconcerned about violating his customary punctuality at the office.

"I am sleepy," Brígida had replied childishly, hiding her face in the pillow.

For once, he rang her up at lunchtime from his club. But she had refused to come to the phone, wielding angrily a weapon she had discovered without thinking: silence.

That same evening she dined across from him with lowered eyes and nerves strung tight.

"Are you still angry, Brígida?"

But she did not answer.

"You know perfectly well that I love you. But I can't be with you all the time. I am a very busy man. When you reach my age, you become a slave to a thousand obligations."

. . .

"Shall we go out tonight?"

. . .

"No? Very well, I will be patient. Tell me, did Roberto call from Montevideo?"

. . .

"What a lovely dress! Is it new?"

. . .

"Is it new, Brígida? Answer me. Say something."

But she refused to break her silence.

And then the unexpected, the astonishing, the absurd. Luis rises from his chair and slaps his napkin on the table, slamming the door as he stomps from the house.

She, too, had gotten to her feet, stunned, trembling with indignation at such injustice. "And I . . . and I . . ." she stammered, "I, who for almost an entire year . . . when for the first time I take the liberty of lodging a complaint . . . Ah, I am leaving—I am leaving this very night! I shall never set foot in this house again . . ." And she jerked open the armoires in her dressing room, strewing clothes furiously in all directions.

It was then that she heard a banging against the windowpane.

She ran to the window and opened it, not knowing how or whence her courage came. It was the rubber tree, set in motion by the storm, knocking its branches on the glass—as though calling her to witness how it twisted and contorted like a fierce black flame under the burning sky of that summer night.

Heavy rain soon began to lash its cold leaves. How lovely! All night long she could hear the rain thrashing, splashing through the leaves of the rubber tree like a thousand tiny rivers sliding down imaginary canals. All night long she heard the ancient trunk creak and moan, the storm raging outside while she curled into a ball between the sheets of the wide bed, very close to Luis.

.

Handfuls of pearls raining on a silver roof. Chopin. *Etudes* by Frédéric Chopin.

How many mornings had she awakened as soon as she sensed that her husband, now likewise maintaining an obstinate silence, had slipped from bed.

Her dressing room: the window thrown wide, the odor of river and grass floating in that hospitable chamber, and the mirrors wearing a veil of fog.

Chopin intermingles in her turbulent memory with rain hissing through the leaves of the rubber tree like some hidden waterfall—so palpable that even the roses on the curtains seem moist.

What to do in summer when it rains so often? Spend the day in her room feigning sadness, a convalescence? One afternoon Luis had entered timidly. Had sat down stiffly. There was a long silence.

"Then it is true, Brígida? You no longer love me?"

A sudden joy seized her. She might have shouted: "No, no. I love you, Luis, I love you," if he had given her time, if he had not almost immediately added, with his habitual calm: "In any case, I do not think it would be convenient for us to separate, Brígida. Such a move requires much thought."

Her impulse sank as fast as it had surfaced. What was the use of exciting herself! Luis loved her tenderly, with moderation; if he ever came to hate her, it would be a just and prudent hatred. And that was life. She walked to the window and placed her forehead against the cold glass. There was the rubber tree, serenely accepting the pelting rain. The room was fixed in shadow, quiet and ordered. Everything seemed to be held in an eternal and very noble equi-

librium. That was life. And there was a certain
grandeur in accepting it thus: mediocre, like some-
thing definite and irremediable. While underneath it
all there seemed to rise a melody of grave and slow
words that transfixed her: "Always. Never" . . .

And in this way the hours, days, and years pass.
Always! Never! Life! Life!

Collecting herself, she realized that her husband
had stolen from the room.

"Always! Never!" . . . And the rain, secret and
steady, still whispered in Chopin.

.

Summer stripped the leaves from its burning calen-
dar. Luminous and blinding pages fell like golden
swords; pages also of malignant dampness like breeze
from a swamp; pages of furious and brief storms, of
hot wind—the wind that carries the "carnation of the
air" and hangs it on the huge rubber tree.

Some children used to play hide-and-seek among
the enormous, twisted roots that pushed up the pav-
ing stones on the sidewalk, and the tree overflowed
with laughter and whispering. On those days she
would look from the window and clap her hands; but
the children dispersed in fear, without noticing the
childlike smile of a girl who wanted to join the game.

Alone, she would lean on her elbows at the window
for a long time, watching the foliage swaying—a
breeze blew along that street which sloped directly to
the river—and it was like staring deep into moving
water or the dancing flames in a fireplace. One could
kill time in this fashion, no need for thought, made
foolish by peace of mind.

She lit the first lamp just as the room began to fill with twilight smoke, and the first lamp flickered in the mirrors, multiplying like fireflies eager to hasten the night.

And night after night she dozed beside her husband, suffering at intervals. But when her pain tightened so that it pierced like a knife thrust, when she was besieged by the desire to wake Luis—to hit him or caress him—she tiptoed to her dressing room and opened the window. Immediately the room came alive with discreet sounds and discreet presences, with mysterious footsteps, the fluttering of wings, the sudden rustling of vegetation, the soft chirping of a cricket perched on the bark of the rubber tree under the stars of a hot summer night.

Little by little her fever went down as her bare feet grew cold on the reed mat. She did not know why it was so easy to suffer in that room.

.

Chopin's melancholy stringing of one *Etude* after another, stringing of one melancholy after another, imperturbably.

And autumn came. The dry leaves hovered an instant before settling on the grass of the narrow garden, on the sidewalk of that sloping street. The leaves came loose and fell . . . The top of the rubber tree remained green but underneath it turned red—darkened like the worn-out lining of a sumptuous evening cape. And now the room seemed to be submerged in a goblet of dull gold.

Lying on the divan, she waited patiently for the dinner hour, and the improbable arrival of Luis. She

had resumed speaking to him, had become his again without enthusiasm or anger. She no longer loved him. But she no longer suffered. On the contrary, an unexpected feeling of fulfillment and placidity had taken hold of her. Nothing, no one could now hurt her. It may be that true happiness lies in the conviction that one has irremediably lost happiness. It is only then that we can begin to live without hope or fear, able finally to enjoy all the small pleasures, which are the most lasting.

A thunderous noise, followed by a flash of light from which she recoils, shaking.

The intermission? No. The rubber tree.

Having started work early in the morning without her knowledge, they had felled it with a single stroke of the ax. "The roots were breaking up the sidewalk, and, naturally, the neighborhood committee . . ."

Dazed, she has shielded her eyes with her hands. When she recovers her sight, she stands and looks around. What does she see?

The concert hall suddenly ablaze with light, the audience filing out?

No. She is imprisoned in the web of her past, trapped in the dressing room—which has been invaded by a terrifying white light. It was as if they had ripped off the roof; a crude light entering from every direction, seeping through her very pores, burning her with its coldness. And she saw everything bathed in that cold light: Luis, his wrinkled face, his hands crisscrossed with ropy discolored veins, and the gaudy cretonnes.

Frightened, she runs to the window. The window

now opens directly on a narrow street, so narrow that her room almost brushes against a shiny skyscraper. On the ground floor, shop windows and more shop windows, full of bottles. At the corner, a row of automobiles lined up in front of a service station painted red. Some boys in their shirtsleeves are kicking a ball in the middle of the street.

And all that ugliness lay embedded in her mirrors, along with nickel-plated balconies, shabby clotheslines, and canary cages.

They had stolen her intimacy, her secret; she found herself naked in the middle of the street, naked before an old husband who turned his back on her in bed, who had given her no children. She does not understand why, until then, she had not wanted children, how she had resigned herself to the idea of life without children. Nor does she comprehend how for a whole year she had tolerated Luis's laughter, that overcheerful laughter, that false laughter of a man who has trained himself in joviality because it is necessary to laugh on certain occasions.

Lies! Her resignation and serenity were lies; she wanted love, yes, love, and trips and madness, and love, love . . .

"But, Brígida—why are you leaving? Why did you stay so long?" Luis had asked.

Now she would have known how to answer him.

"The tree, Luis, the tree! They have cut down the rubber tree."

Braids

Day by day, proud human beings that we are, we have a tendency to renounce our elemental roots, which accounts for the fact that women no longer appreciate their braids.

Being rationalists nowadays, women in cutting off their braids ignore that in effect they are severing their ties with those magic currents which issue from the very heart of the earth.

Because a woman's hair springs from the most profound and mysterious source, whence is born the first trembling seed of life—evolving therefrom to struggle and grow among many entangling forces, thrusting through the vegetal surface into the air and on upwards to the privileged forehead of its choice.

Did not the dark and lustrous braids of Isolde, princess of Ireland, absorb this mysterious power even as her lips took the first drop of that enchanted potion?

Was it not owing perhaps to the length of her braids that the potion led her so swiftly to her fate? For there is no doubt that her swirling hair murmured like underground fountains, sighed like the breeze whispering through leaves. Murmur and sighing— which held Tristram spellbound on those nights of moonlight and love, when he undid her tresses and listened in ecstasy to the far-off singing, persistent and secret . . . the song of nature emanating from her hair.

And I know that even when Isolde was asleep her tousled hair maintained its power—on the elegant pillows of Tintagel Castle as well as in the wheat fields of exile . . . and her braids blossomed from those exotic flowers that she uprooted in fear with every dawn.

.

And Queen Mélisande's blond braids, longer even than her delicate body.

Braids that, as she leaned over her tower in the autumn twilight, came to rest imprudently on the strong shoulders of the king's brother.

"Mélisande," Pelléas cries in awe. Then, quaking, daring at last to let his heart speak: "Mélisande," he murmurs, "your braids, I can finally touch your braids, kiss them, enfold myself in them."

In answer—only a sigh from the top of the tower. The braids had already unwittingly confessed that shy and timid truth their owner was hiding within her heart.

.

And why not at this point recall the braids of our sweet María from the novel by Jorge Isaacs? Disembodied braids wrapped in that blue apron she wore when watering her small garden.

Braids covered with dried butterflies and memories which slept under Efraín's pillow during his long night of grief.

Dead braids, and yet somehow a living testament that obliged him to go on living, if only to remember her.

Bluebeard's eighth wife—have you forgotten her?
Forgotten how her severe and extravagant husband,
before leaving on an unexpected journey, entrusted
his mischievous young bride with the keys to every
chamber in that vast and sumptuous mansion, pro-
hibiting only the use of that rusty little key which
opened the last room in a forbidding and uncarpeted
corridor?

Needless to say, during this welcome marital sepa-
ration, in the midst of much amusement, laughing
friends, and genteel courtiers, the game that intrigued
and tempted her the most was the only game for-
bidden: inserting that mysterious little key into the
lock of that innermost, abandoned room.

Now, it is well known that, in women as well as
cats, curiosity dominates all other passions. And so,
when her lord and master returned without warning,
the disobedient, quivering wife surrendered the keys,
among them one the fearful knight, in spite of her
attempts to disguise it, found not only rusty but
flecked with blood.

"You, my lady, have betrayed me!" he roared. "For
which your fate shall be to join your wretched prede-
cessors at the end of the corridor."

Having said this, he unsheathed his sword . . .

And what is the relevance of this old story that we
learn in our childhood, you must be wondering. It
has nothing to do with braids . . .

Ah, but it does! I reply vehemently. You fail to
understand that what saved her was not the brief

reprieve granted by her enraged husband to say her last prayers; nor was it her pleading, or the terrified cries the frightened Anne sent forth from the tower, beseeching help for her sister.

Nor was it the coincidental appearance of her two warrior brothers, who at that very moment were riding toward the castle for a visit.

No, none of these circumstances saved her.

It was her braids, and only her braids, intricately wound in a hundred silky, capricious coils that, when her implacable husband threw her brutally at his feet to consummate his crime, seized and obstructed his murderous fingers so that he found himself snarled up to the sword hilt in those desperate curls protecting her delicate head until the providential arrival of the aforementioned warriors, her well-beloved brothers, who had been invited earlier by our curious heroine.

You must admit it was not in vain that during her innocent and happy youth the girl who later became the foolish Castilian and last wife of Bluebeard sang as she brushed her hair, endowing it with vigor and beauty.

.

"She was very pale, like those women who have long hair," Balzac describes one of his enigmatic heroines.

And that was no verbal caprice.

Because undoubtedly Balzac must have been blessed with an intuition of the ultimate relationship that can exist between human beings and the profound mystery of the earth.

And I am here to verify and illustrate his affirmation with a tale of a strange event witnessed by so many of us only a few years ago.

Of what use are names and places? Those who are familiar know; the rest can guess.

.

Two sisters.

The declining days of an old, brilliant, powerful family—albeit one amply beset by hidden passions, unexpected deaths, and suicides.

The older sister, who since her youth had endured a loveless existence, cut her hair short one day, dressed herself in a simple poncho made of vicuña wool, and, in spite of her parents' grief-stricken protests, retired to the family's large southern hacienda—which she was determined to administer with an iron hand. The gentle country people soon named her the Amazon. She was stubborn but fair. Ugly but with an aristocratic carriage and a generous smile. A spinster . . . no one knew why.

By contrast, the younger sister had become a widow voluntarily—having shot her adulterous husband out of wounded pride. She was very beautiful, but suffered from extremely fragile health.

She also lived alone, in the family's old mansion in the city. She had a soft voice, quiet brown eyes, but the single red braid that she wore in a circlet around her small head cast a resplendent light over her pale complexion.

Yes, she was a sweet and terrible woman. She would fall in love and love madly.

.

It all began on the hacienda that autumn night when the gamekeeper ran down to the dale shouting: "Fire!"

For some time, however, her forehead pressed against the windowpane, the Amazon had been gazing with fascination at that precocious and purple dawn beginning to blaze up there on her hills . . . Then, in her usual calm manner, she gave the necessary instructions to the servants of the manor, ordered her horse brought, and set off toward the fire, accompanied by her foremen.

.

Meanwhile, in the city, the younger sister, just returned from a ball, lay on the rug of the salon, victim of a sudden faint.

Her suitors were gone, her servants asleep, she was hidden in the shadow of the candelabra she had been in the act of extinguishing. Like a devious accomplice, a gust of cold wind stirred the balcony drapes, billowing them, to settle on the defenseless woman's forehead, shoulders, and exposed breasts.

.

In the southern hacienda, the Amazon and her retinue were climbing the hills, penetrating the woods, the fires. Another blast of wind, hot and acrid, swept over them, carrying a cloud of scorched leaves, blinded birds, burning nests.

She knew beforehand that she was beaten. No one could have stopped the fury of those flames.

Later, sitting on the trunk of a dead tree that had fallen many years ago, the Amazon stoically resigned

herself to the distant spectacle of the catastrophe, with the sullen dignity of a despised millionaire witnessing the ransacking and destruction of his riches.

The forest was burning almost silently before her eyes, trees falling one by one, row after row, like the columns of a familiar cathedral, while, as in a dream, she contemplated her loss . . . thinking, remembering, allowing herself, after so many years, to suffer . . .

That enormous hazelnut tree being consumed . . . Hadn't her brothers and sisters gathered with their governess under its avalanche of hard fruit to enjoy their special picnics?

And behind that gigantic trunk, I forget its name, she would run to hide after a prank . . . and those little mushrooms they used to pick under the cedar . . . and that eucalyptus she had embraced—very young, crying stupidly after experiencing her first disillusionment: that grief she never confessed, that pain which drove her to cut her hair, to become the Amazon, resolving never to love again . . . never . . .

.

There, in the city, dawn was breaking over the carpet on which lay the still form of her sister—the one who dared to love—sinking gradually, with gentle spasms, into what is called death, unseen, beyond help . . . though her red braid was still vivid, seemingly alive.

And suddenly, down there on the hacienda, the final act: the exodus of brave horses returning with singed hair standing on end, having saved their almost asphyxiated riders.

From the immense ruined forest rose enormous tongues of smoke, climbing high and straight as the trees which had once stood there.

And for a brief moment the ghost of a forest wavered before the eyes of the owner and her weeping servants. She did not cry, however.

Then: debris, ashes, silence.

.

When they came to close the balcony doors and carry the fragile woman to her bed, trying in vain to revive her, to warm her, it was too late.

The doctor concluded that she had taken all night to die.

You see, the forest had to die along with her and her hair, because they shared the same roots.

.

Because the green climbing plants that twine on the trees, the sweet algae clinging to the rocks, are but strands of hair: are the word, the coming and soaring of nature—its happiness and melancholy, the means of expression by which she gently instills her magic and wisdom into all living things.

.

And it is for this reason that women nowadays, having renounced their braids, have lost their prophetic powers, no longer have premonitions, or feel absurd joy, or have their old magnetism.

And as a result their dreams are but a sad sea tide bringing and rebringing faded images, or some other domestic nightmare.

The Unknown

For Shannon Patricia Cunningham—
so pretty and intelligent,
and such a good little girl

I am privy to much that is unknown.

Of sea and earth and sky I know an infinity of small and magic secrets.

This time, however, I will tell only about the sea.

Miles down, below the deep, dense zone of darkness, the ocean again illuminates itself. A golden light radiates from gigantic sponges, yellow and resplendent as suns.

Numberless plants and cold-blooded creatures live within this layer of light, buried eternally in the brightness of a glacial summer.

A profusion of green and red anemones blossom on the wide sandy lawn, amid schools of transparent jellyfish, dangling like umbrellas, which have not yet set out in quest of their wandering destiny through the seas.

Hard white corals entwine like bushes, through which glide dark velvet fish, opening and closing like flowers.

Sea horses there are: tiny thoroughbreds of the deep moving at a silent canter with radiant algae manes rising slowly round them like halos.

And only I know that underneath certain deformed conch shells burrowed on the bottom there sits a little mermaid, weeping.

Surely you remember when as children we would

leap from rock to rock, stopping short to balance with our arms widespread like wings on the edge of a narrow crevice carved by the sea—a jagged inlet where the waves crashed and then, retreating, left in their wake a long, foaming mantle: iridescent, gliding through the spectrum on its reluctant return, hissing, hissing . . . whispering something like a message.

But did you understand the meaning of that message?

Well, I did.

For in fact the foam was trying with its dying breath to whisper in our ear the secret of its noble origins . . .

"Far, far away, deep in the ocean depths," sighed the foam, "there exists a submarine volcano erupting ceaselessly. Night and day the crater boils, blowing dense bubbles of silver lava toward the surface . . ."

But I digress. My primary objective in these brief lines is to acquaint you with something strange and until now unknown which likewise took place down there in the abyss.

It is the tale of a pirate ship trapped centuries ago in the vortex of a whirlpool that sent it spinning to the bottom amid uncharted currents and buried reefs.

Time passed. Giant octopuses tugged gently at the topmasts as if to set a new course. Starfish came to nestle in the hold.

Recovering at last from his long swoon, the pirate captain roused his crew with a roar and gave the order to weigh anchor.

And as the dazed seamen raced to man the capstan,

the captain went to the bridge—where no sooner had he taken in his surroundings than he began to curse.

For the ship had run aground on an endless beach bathed in dark-green moonlight.

To make matters worse, regardless of what direction he turned his telescope, there was no sign of water.

"Damned sea!" he shouted. "Blasted tides driven by the devil himself. Thunder take them for leaving us stranded so far inland . . . Who knows how long before they'll lift us off this bloody beach."

He turned, training the telescope overhead to inspect the sky, the stars, the position of that eerily glowing moon.

But his eyes encountered neither sky nor stars nor visible moon; rather, what he saw was the exact inverted reflection of that demonic, sandy desert on which the ship was marooned. "In the name of Satan," he whispered, "am I going mad?"

And then, to top things off, he noticed one final oddity: the luxuriant black sails—the pride of his ship—though motionless and silent, were bellying full from every mast . . . yet not a breath of wind was blowing.

"Ashore all hands!" rang suddenly throughout the ship. "Load weapons, keep your cutlasses at the ready, and scout this cursed coast!"

The gangplank promptly lowered, a groggy crew disembarks, followed by their captain with a pistol in his hand.

They sank ankle-deep in the fine, cold, silky sand.

Two groups they formed: one plodding east, the other west—both in search of the sea.

Then abruptly, "Halt!" the captain bellowed. "Chico will stay here to guard the ship. Now the rest of you swabs hop to it. On the double!"

And Chico—a mere lad, son of an honest fisherman, who had run away from home in search of adventure and mischief—upon hearing the command trudged back to the ship with his head bowed, as if counting each one of his steps.

"Dunderhead! . . . bandy-legged son of a Dutchman! . . . turtlebrain!" the captain ranted when the boy stood before him—so small, in spite of his fifteen years, that he scarcely reached the solid-gold buckle on the captain's bloodstained belt.

Children on board, he thought to himself, struck by a sudden uneasiness.

"Captain," the boy said quietly, "have you noticed that our feet leave no tracks in this sand?"

"Nor do the sails throw any shadow," the captain added in a dry, cruel whisper.

Then, his anger seeming to abate before the boy's naïve and puzzled gaze, he laid his rough hand on Chico's shoulder and said, "Let's go, son. The tide will be in soon."

"Aye aye, sir," the boy murmured, as though he meant "thanks."

Thanks. Forbidden word among pirates. Sooner burn your lips than utter it.

Did I say thanks? Chico asks himself, startled.

I called him son, the captain realized in amazement.

"Captain," Chico began, "at the time of the ship-
wreck . . ." He faltered as the captain bristled,
blinked, raising himself to his full height. "I mean,
the accident . . . well, I was in the hold. When I came
to my senses, what do you think I found? Myself
surrounded by the most disgusting creatures I've ever
seen."

"What kind of creatures?"

"Well, starfish . . . but alive. And gross. Quivering
like the insides of someone just disemboweled . . .
slithering from one side to the other, piling up in
slippery mounds, even trying to fasten onto me . . ."

"Ha! And you were frightened, eh?"

"Quick as an eel I jumped up and jerked open the
doors and the aft hatchways, kicking them and swat-
ting them with the broom as I swept them out. How
like crabs they scuttled across the sand! But one thing
I must tell you, sir, is that *they* left tracks."

The captain makes no reply.

And for a time both stood there side by side under
that deathly green light, amid a silence so complete
that suddenly they began to hear.

To hear and feel within themselves the surge and
rise of an unknown tide, the pull of a sentiment
neither could give a name to, a sentiment far more
destructive than anger or hatred or dread—an orderly
sentiment, nocturnal, gnawing, to which the heart,
patient and resigned, surrenders.

Like one entranced, Chico at last whispers, "Sad-
ness," as though it were a new word just breathed in
his ear.

And then the captain, trying to shake off the nightmare, reverted to his loud voice. "Enough, Chico. Let's talk plain. With us you learned to fight, to wield a dagger, to sack and burn . . . but I've never heard you blaspheme." He paused and then, lowering his voice, asked: "Tell me, you must know—where do you believe we are?"

"Exactly where you think we are, Captain," the boy answered respectfully.

"In that case," the pirate said with a loud and scornful laugh, "thousands of fathoms beneath the sea and damned." A second later the laughter died in his throat.

Because what he had intended as mirth echoed like a terrifying moan, a cry of affliction from someone desperate, burning with desire for something irrevocably lost.

New Islands

All night long a howling wind had raged across the pampa. Now and then it would slip inside the house through cracks in the doors and window frames, sending ripples through the mosquito netting. Each time this happened, Yolanda would turn on the light, which flickered, held for a moment, and then faded out again. At dawn, when her brother Federico came into the room, she lay on her left shoulder, breathing with difficulty, moaning in her sleep.

"Yolanda! Yolanda!"

She sat up like a shot. In order to see Federico, she parted her long black hair and tossed it over her shoulders.

"Were you dreaming?" he asked.

"Oh, yes—horrible dreams."

"Why must you always sleep in that position? It's bad for your heart."

"I know, I know. What time is it? And where are you off to so early in all this wind?"

"The lakes. It seems another island has emerged. That makes four so far. Some people from La Figura hacienda have come to see them. So we'll be having guests later. I wanted to let you know before I left."

Without shifting her position, Yolanda regarded her brother: a thin, white-haired man whose tight-

fitting riding boots lent him an air of youth. Men—
how absurd they were! Always in motion, forever
willing to take an interest in everything. Upon re-
tiring for the night, they demand to be awakened at
daybreak. If they go to a fireplace, they remain stand-
ing, ready to run to the other end of the room—
ready always to escape, to flee toward the futile. And
they cough and smoke, speak loud as if they feared
silence—indeed, as if tranquillity were a mortal
enemy.

"It's all right, Federico."

"So long, then."

The door slams; Federico's spurs jingle on the tile
floor in the corridor. Yolanda closes her eyes once
more and, delicately, using elaborate care, sinks back
onto the pillows on her left shoulder, curling herself
as usual into that position which Federico claims is
so damaging to one's heart. Breathing heavily, she
sighs, falling suddenly into one of her disturbing
dreams—dreams from which, morning after morning,
she wakes pale and exhausted, as if she had been
battling insomnia throughout the entire night.

The visitors from La Figura hacienda, meanwhile,
had reached the grassy bank where the lakes began.
Daylight was spreading across the water, unfurling
over the landscape like a fire. Out there against the
horizon, barely visible under the cloudy sky, were
the new islands: still smoking from the fiery effort
that had lifted them from who knows what stratified
depths.

"Four, four new islands!" the people shouted.

The wind did not subside until nightfall, by which time the men were returning from hunting.

Do, re, mi, fa, sol, la, ti, do . . . Do, re, mi, fa, sol, la, ti, do . . .

The notes rise and fall, rise and fall like round, limpid crystal bubbles carried on the wind from the house, now flattened in the distance, to burst over the hunters like solemn, regulated raindrops.

Do, re, mi, fa, sol, la, ti, do . . .

It's Yolanda practicing, Sylvester says to himself. He pauses a moment to shift the carbine slung on his left shoulder, his heavy body trembling slightly.

Among the bushes bordering the lawn there are white flowers that appear touched by frost. Juan Manuel bends over to examine one.

"Don't touch them," Sylvester warns. "They turn yellow. They're Yolanda's camellias," he adds with a smile.

That humble smile which does not suit him, thinks Juan Manuel. As soon as he relaxes his proud countenance, you see how old he is.

The house is in total darkness, but the notes continue to flow regularly: Do, re, mi, fa, sol, la, ti, do . . . Do, re, mi, fa, sol, la, ti, do . . .

"Have you met my sister Yolanda, Juan Manuel?"

On Federico's question, the woman sitting in shadow at the piano gives the stranger her hand, withdrawing it immediately. She then rises, so slowly that she seems to grow upright, uncoiling like a beautiful snake. Very tall, she is extremely slender.

Juan Manuel follows her with his eyes as she quickly and quietly turns on the lamps.

She is exactly like her name, thinks Juan Manuel. Pale, angular, and a bit savage. And there is something odd about her that I cannot place. But of course, he realizes as she glides through the door and disappears—her feet are too small. How strange that she can support such a long body on such tiny feet.

.

How dull this dinner among men, Juan Manuel decides. Among ten hunters thwarted by the wind who gulp down their food without a single manly deed to boast about. And Yolanda, he reflects, why doesn't she preside over the table now that Federico's wife is in Buenos Aires? What an extraordinary figure she makes! Ugly? Pretty? Fragile, that's it, very fragile. And that dark and brilliant gaze of hers— aggressive yet hunted . . . Whom does she look like? What does she resemble?

Juan Manuel lifts his glass, staring at the wine. Across from him sits Sylvester, who is drinking heavily and talking and laughing in a loud voice. He seems desperate.

The hunters stir the coals with a scoop and tongs, scattering ashes over the multiple fiery eyes which refuse to close—this the final act in a long and boring evening.

And now suddenly the grass and the trees in the garden begin to shiver in the cold night breeze. Large insects beat their wings against the lantern illuminating the long open corridor. Leaning on Juan

Manuel, Sylvester staggers toward his room, his feet slipping on the tiles that shine with vapor as if they had just been washed. His footsteps send frogs scurrying off to hide timidly in dark corners.

The iron grilles slamming shut across the doors seem in the silence of the night to echo the useless volley of shots fired by the hunters. Sylvester throws his heavy body on the bed and buries his emaciated face in his hands. His sighs irritate Juan Manuel— he who always detested sharing a room with anyone, let alone with a drunkard who moans.

"Oh, Juan Manuel, Juan Manuel . . ."

"What's the matter, Don Sylvester? You don't feel well?"

"Oh, my boy—who could know, who could know! . . ."

"Know what, Don Sylvester?"

"This," said the old man, taking his wallet from his jacket and handing it to Juan Manuel. "Look for the letter. Read it. Yes, a letter. That one, yes. Read it and tell me if you understand it."

An elongated, wavering handwriting flows like smoke across the yellowed, wrinkled pages: *Sylvester, I cannot marry you. Believe me, I have thought it over at great length. It isn't possible, it just isn't. Nevertheless, I love you, Sylvester, I love you and I suffer. But I cannot. Forget me. In vain I ask myself what might save me. A son, perhaps, a child whose sweet weight I could feel inside me forever. Forever! Not to see him grow, separated from me! Myself attached forever to that tiny heart, possessed always by*

that presence! I weep, Sylvester, I weep; and I cannot explain myself. —Yolanda.

"I don't understand," Juan Manuel whispers uneasily.

"I have been trying for thirty years to understand," said Sylvester. "I loved her. You cannot know how much I loved her. No one loves like that any more, Juan Manuel . . . One night, two weeks before we were to be married, she sent me this letter. Afterwards she refused to offer any explanation, and I was never permitted to see her alone. I waited, telling myself that time would solve everything. I am still waiting."

Juan Manuel seemed confused. "Was it the mother, Don Sylvester? Was she also named Yolanda?"

"What? I am speaking of the one and only Yolanda, who tonight has again rejected me. This evening when I saw her, I said to myself: Maybe now that so many years have passed, Yolanda will at long last give me an explanation. But, as usual, she left the room. Sometimes, you know, Federico tries to talk to her about all this. But she starts trembling and runs away, as always . . ."

The far-off chugging of a train can now be heard. The steady insistent clacking seems to increase Juan Manuel's uneasiness.

"Yolanda was your fiancée, Don Sylvester?"

"Yes, my fiancée . . . my fiancée . . ."

Juan Manuel stares coldly at Sylvester's disoriented gestures, his swollen, sixty-year-old body so disas-

trously preserved. Don Sylvester, his father's old friend, and Yolanda's fiancé.

"Then she is not a young girl, Don Sylvester?"

Sylvester laughs stupidly.

"How old is she?" Juan Manuel inquires.

Sylvester rubs his forehead, eyes closed, trying to count. "Let's see, at that time I was twenty . . . no, twenty-three . . ."

But Juan Manuel hardly listens, momentarily relieved by a consoling reflection: What does age matter when one is so prodigiously young!

"Therefore she must be . . ."

Sylvester's words dissolve in a hacking cough. And again Juan Manuel feels a resurgence of the anxiety that holds him attentive to the secret Sylvester is drunkenly unraveling. And that train in the distance, coming closer now, its regular rhythm as laden with suspense as a drum roll—like a threat not yet become reality. The muffled, monotonous pounding unnerves him, growing louder and louder until, like one seeking escape, he goes to the window, pushes it open, and bends into the night. The headlights of the express glare across the immense plain like malevolent eyes.

"Damned train!" he grumbles. "When will it pass?"

Sylvester comes over to lean beside him, breathing deep as he gestures toward the two shimmering lights.

"It just left Lobos," he explains. "It generally takes half an hour to go by here."

She is fragile and her feet are too small for her height.

"How old is she, Don Sylvester?"

"I don't remember. I'll tell you tomorrow."

But why? Juan Manuel asks himself. Why this pre-occupation with a woman I have seen only once in my life? Do I desire her? The train. Oh, that monotonous hissing monster advancing slowly, inexorably across the pampa! What's wrong with me? It must be that I am tired, he thinks, closing the window.

.

Meanwhile, she is at one end of the garden, leaning against the fence overlooking the hill as if she were bending over the rail of a ship anchored on the prairie. In the sky, a single motionless star: a large red star that seems about to shake loose from its orbit and spin off into infinite space. Juan Manuel stands beside her at the fence, gazing, too, at the pampa now submerged in the dark saturnine twilight. He speaks. What does he say? He whispers words of destiny in her ear. And now he takes her in his arms. And now the arms around her waist tremble, slide lower, caressing her gently. And she tosses, struggles, gripping the wooden rail to better resist. And then she wakes to find herself clutching the sheets, sobbing deep in her throat.

For a long time she weeps without moving, listening to the house quaver. The mirror moves slightly. A withered camellia blossom falls from a vase, dropping on the carpet with the soft thick sound of ripe fruit.

She waits for the train to go by and then, listening to its receding sonic boom, she drifts back to sleep, lying on her left shoulder.

.

In the morning the wind has resumed its fierce race across the pampa. But this day the hunters are in no mood to waste their ammunition in a gale. Instead, they launch two boats, bound for those new islands afloat on the horizon, rising from a cloud of foam and wheeling birds.

They land proudly, boisterously, carbines on their shoulders as they leap to shore, only to discover an oppressive, foul-smelling atmosphere that stops them in their tracks. After a brief pause they advance, stepping in amazement on slimy weeds that seem to be oozing from the hot and shifting soil. They stagger on amid spirals of sea gulls that swoop around them, flashing by their faces and screeching as they dip and rise. At one point, Juan Manuel lurches as the edge of a wing flails his chest.

And still they advance, crushing under their boots frenzied silver fish stranded by the tide. Farther on, they find more strange vegetation: low bushes of pink coral, which they struggle for some time to uproot, pulling and pulling until their hands bleed.

The sea gulls cluster round them in ever-tightening spirals. Low, running clouds skim by overhead, weaving a vertiginous pattern of shadows. The fumes rising from the earth grow more dense by the moment. Everything boils, shakes violently, trembles. The hunters cannot see; can hardly breathe. Disheartened and afraid, they flee to their boats, return in silence to the mainland.

All afternoon they sat around a bonfire, chatting with the peons who periodically fed the flames with

eucalyptus branches, waiting for the wind to abate. But again, as if to exasperate them, the wind did not die down until dusk.

Do, re, mi, fa, sol, la, ti, do . . . Once again, that methodical scale drifts toward them from the house. Juan Manuel pricks up his ears.

Do, re, mi, fa, sol, la, ti, do . . . Do, re, mi, fa, sol, la, ti, do . . . Do, re, mi, fa . . . Do, re, mi, fa . . . —the piano insists. And those notes repeated over and over beat against Juan Manuel's heart, striking where the sea gull's wing had wounded him that morning. Without knowing why, he gets to his feet and starts walking toward that music chiming endlessly through the trees like a summons.

As he reaches the camellia bushes, the piano suddenly falls silent. He enters the darkened drawing room almost at a run, sees logs burning in the fireplace, the piano open . . . But where is Yolanda?

At the far end of the garden she leans against the fence, as if resting on the rail of a ship anchored on the pampa. And now she trembles, hearing the rustle of the lowermost pine-tree branches being brushed aside by someone coming up cautiously behind her. If only it were Juan Manuel!

She slowly turns her head. It is him, in the flesh this time. Oh, his dark, golden complexion in the gray twilight! Golden as though he were enveloped by a sunray. Joining her at the fence, he, too, stares out across the pampa. Frogs begin to sing in the irrigation ditches; and it is as if night were being ushered in by thousands of crystal bells.

Now he looks at her and smiles. Oh, his fine white teeth! They must be cold and hard like tiny chips of ice. And that warm virile odor he gives off, piercing her with pleasure. How sad to resist such pleasure, to shun that circle formed by this strong, beautiful man and his shadow!

"Yolanda," he murmurs.

She feels upon hearing her name that a sudden intimacy exists between them. How marvelous that he called her by name! It would seem that now they are linked by a long and passionate past. Not sharing a past—that was what held them apart and inhibited them.

"All night long I dreamed of you, Juan Manuel, all night long . . ."

He embraces her; she does not reject him. But she obliges his arm to remain chastely around her waist.

"Someone is calling me," she says abruptly, moving out of his embrace and running off. The pine branches she hastily brushes aside rebound with a snap in Juan Manuel's face, scratching his cheek. Disconcerted by a woman for the first time in his life, he runs after her.

She is dressed in white. Only now, as she goes over to her brother to light his pipe—gravely and meticulously, as if performing a trifling daily ritual—only now does he notice that she is wearing a long gown. She has put it on to dine with them. Then Juan Manuel remembers the mud on his boots and rushes to his room to clean them.

On his return to the drawing room, he finds Yolanda seated on a sofa in front of the fireplace. The dancing flames alternately lighten and darken her black eyes. With her arms crossed behind her neck, she is long and slender like a sword, or like . . . like what? In vain Juan Manuel searches for the proper simile.

"Dinner is served," the maid announces.

As Yolanda rises, her flame-lightened pupils are suddenly extinguished. And going past Juan Manuel, she casts those opaque black eyes on him, the sheer tulle sleeve of her dress grazing his chest like a wing. And in that instant the simile comes to him.

"Now I know what you look like," he whispers. "A sea gull."

Uttering a strange, hoarse cry, Yolanda collapses on the carpet. Momentarily stunned, the others now rush to her side, pick her up, carry her unconscious form to the sofa. Federico sends the maid scurrying for water. Turning angrily to Juan Manuel, he asks: "What did you say to her? What did you *say?*"

"I told her . . ." Juan Manuel begins; then lapses into silence, feeling a sudden stab of guilt—fearing, without knowing why, to reveal a secret which is not his.

Yolanda, meanwhile, comes to. Sighing, she presses her heart with both hands, as if recovering from a fright. She half sits up, then stretches out on her left shoulder.

"No," Federico protests, "not on your heart. It's bad for you."

She gives him a weak smile, whispers as she waves him away: "I know, I know. Now please leave me alone."

And there is such sad vehemence, such weariness in her gesture, that everyone moves off into the next room without objecting—everyone except Juan Manuel, who remains standing beside the fireplace.

Pale and motionless, Yolanda sleeps, or pretends to sleep, while Juan Manuel, a silent sentinel, waits anxiously for a sign—be it to stay or go.

.

At daybreak on this third morning the hunters gather once more at the edge of the lakes, which today at last are calm. Mute, they contemplate the smooth surface of the water, shocked into silence by the vista on that distant gray horizon.

For the new islands have vanished.

Again they launch boats, Juan Manuel setting off alone in a dinghy. He rows determinedly, skirting the old islands, which teem with wildlife, refusing to be tempted like his companions by the lashing sound of wings, of cooing and small sharp cries—the old islands, where things rattle and crack like rattan splitting, where the banks are covered with oozy moving flowers spread out like a bed of slime. Soon Juan Manuel is lost in the distance, a receding silhouette rowing a zigzagging course in search of the exact spot where only yesterday they had landed to explore the four new islands. Where was the first one? Here. No, there. No, rather, here. He leans over the water to look for it, though he knows that his eyes could never

see the muddy bottom, where, after its vertiginous plunge, the island sank into silt and algae.

Within the circle of a nearby whirlpool something soft and transparent floats: a small jellyfish. Plucking it from the water in his handkerchief, Juan Manuel ties the four corners of the cloth over it like a pouch.

.

The day is drawing to a close when Yolanda brings her horse to a halt at the base of the hill and opens the gate for the returning hunters. Setting off again, she rides on ahead to the house, the skirt of her tweed riding habit brushing the bushes. And Juan Manuel notes that, though she is mounted in the old-fashioned way, sitting genteelly sidesaddle, with her hair streaming around her face she looks like an Amazon huntress. The light is fading fast, giving way to a dusky bluish spectrum. A chorus of long-tailed magpies croaks by overhead before fluttering down on the naked branches of the now ashen forest.

Juan Manuel suddenly recalls a painting that still hangs in the corridor of his old hacienda in Adrogué: a tall, pensive Amazon equestrienne who, having surrendered to her horse's will, seems to wander lost and disheartened among dry leaves at dusk. The picture is entitled "Autumn," or "Sadness"—he does not remember which.

On the night table in his room he finds a letter from his mother. *Since you are not here, I will take the orchid for Elsa tomorrow*, she writes. Tomorrow. That is today, he realizes. Today, then, is the fifth anniversary of his wife's death. Five years already.

Her name was Elsa. He had never grown accustomed to the fact that she had such a lovely name. "And your name is *Elsa*," he would say as he embraced her, as if that alone were a miracle more breathtaking even than her fair beauty and placid smile. Elsa! The perfection of her features! Her translucent complexion, under which ran veins that seemed the fine blue strokes of a master watercolorist. So many years of love! And then that deadly disease. Like a piercing knife comes the memory of that night when, covering her face with her hands to ward off his kiss, she had cried: "I don't want you to see me like this, so ugly . . . not even after death. You must cover my face with orchids. You have to promise me . . ."

But Juan Manuel does not want to begin thinking of all that. Desolate, he tosses the letter on the night table without reading further.

.

The same serene twilight suffusing the pampa washes over Buenos Aires, inundating in steel blue the stones and the air and the mist-covered trees in Recoleta Square.

Juan Manuel's mother walks confidently through a labyrinth of narrow streets. Never has she lost her way in this intricate city, for as a child her parents taught her how to find her bearings in any quarter. And here is their dwelling—the small cold crypt where parents, grandparents, and so many ancestors rest. So many in such a narrow chamber! If only it were true that each of them sleeps alone with his past and his present, isolated yet side by side! But no,

that isn't possible. She lays her spray of orchids on the ground, rummaging through her purse for the key. Then, before the altar, she makes the sign of the cross and checks that the candelabra are well polished, that the white altar cloth is well starched. She sighs and descends into the crypt, holding nervously on to the bronze railing. An oil lamp hangs from the low ceiling, its flame mirrored in the black marble floor and shining on the bronze rings of the various compartments arranged sequentially by date. Here all is order and solemn indifference.

Outside, the drizzle starts up again. The raindrops rebound audibly on the concrete streets. But here everything seems remote: the rain, the city, the obligations that await her at home. And now she sighs again, going over to the smallest and newest compartment, and places the orchids at the head of the casket—where Elsa's face reposes. Poor Juan Manuel, she thinks.

She tries unsuccessfully to feel sadness for her daughter-in-law's fate. But that rancor she admits only to the priest persists in her heart, despite the dozens of rosaries and the multiple short prayers her confessor orders her to recite as penance.

She stares hard at the casket, wishing her eyes could pierce the metal liner, wanting to see, to know, to verify . . . Dead for five years! She was so fragile. Perhaps the plain gold ring has already slipped off her frivolous crumbling fingers, fallen into that dusty hole that was once her bosom. Maybe so. But is she dead? No. She has won in spite of everything. One

never dies entirely, that is the truth. That strong
dark little boy who continues their line, the grandson
who has become her only reason for living, has the
blue and candid eyes of Elsa.

.

At three o'clock in the morning Juan Manuel
finally resolves to abandon the armchair beside the
fireplace where, nearly stupefied by the heat of the
flames, he has been smoking and drinking listlessly
for hours. He hops over the dogs asleep in the door-
way and starts down the long, open corridor. He feels
lazy and tired, very tired. Last night Sylvester, he
thinks, and tonight me. I am completely drunk.

Sylvester is asleep. He must have dropped off unex-
pectedly, because the lamp on the night table is still
lit.

His mother's letter lies where he left it, still half
open. A long postscript scribbled by his son brings a
brief smile to his lips. He tries to decipher the wind-
ing infantile handwriting through blurred eyes: *Papá.
Grandma says I can write to you here. I have learned
three more words from the new geography book you
gave me. And I am going to write the words and the
definitions from memory.*

*Aerolite: Name given to pieces of minerals that fall
from outer space to the earth's surface. Aerolites are
planetary fragments that float in space and . . .*

"Aiee!" Juan Manuel moans to himself, staggering
as he shakes his head to blot out the definition, those
evocative, dazzling words that blind him as though

a thousand tiny suns were bursting in front of his eyes.

Hurricane: Violent swirling wind made up of various opposing air masses that form whirlwinds . . .

"That boy!" Juan Manuel groans. And he feels chilled to the bone, while a tremendous roaring pounds his brain like icy waves pounding a beach.

Halo: Luminous circle that sometimes surrounds the moon.

A light mist seeping through the open window obscures his vision, a blue mist that enfolds him softly. "Halo," he murmurs. An immense tenderness comes over him. Yolanda! If only he could see her, talk to her!

If only he could stand at her bedroom door and listen to her breathing.

Everyone, everything is asleep. How many doors he had to open, some by force, as he crept across the east wing of that old hacienda, hooding the lamp flame with his cupped hand! How many empty, dusty rooms where furniture lay piled in the corners, and how many others in which, as he passed by, unrecognizable people sighed and turned under the sheets!

He had chosen the way of ghosts and murderers.

And now that he has his ear against Yolanda's door, all he can hear is the beating of his own heart.

A piece of furniture must, no doubt, block the door from the inside; a very light piece of furniture, since he shoves it aside with little effort. Who is moaning?

Juan Manuel turns up the lamp; the room at first seems to spin, then becomes quiet and orderly as his eyes adjust.

He sees a narrow bed veiled by mosquito netting where Yolanda sleeps on her left side, her dark curly hair covering her face like a latticework of luxuriant vines. She moans, caught in some nightmare. Juan Manuel sets the lamp on the floor, parts the mosquito netting, and takes her hand. She clutches his fingers as he helps her to rise from the pillows, to escape from the dream and the weight of that monstrous hair which must have pinned her down in those dark regions of sleep.

She opens her eyes at last, sighs with relief, and whispers: "Thank you."

"Thank you," she repeats, fixing him with her somnambulant eyes. "Oh, it was awful!" she explains. "I was in a horrible place. In a park I often visit in my sleep. A park. Giant plants. Ferns tall as trees. And silence . . . I don't know how to describe it . . . Silence as green as chloroform . . . and suddenly, beneath the silence, a low buzzing sound, growing louder, coming nearer . . . Death, it is death. And then I tried to escape, to wake up. Because if I did not wake up, if death ever found me in that park, I would be doomed to stay forever, don't you think?"

Juan Manuel makes no reply, fearing to shatter this intimacy with the sound of his voice.

Taking a deep breath, Yolanda continues. "They say that in sleep we return to those places where we lived in a prior existence. I, too, sometimes return to a

certain Creole house. A room, a patio, a room, another patio with a fountain in the center. I go there and . . ."

She falls silent and looks at him.

The moment he feared so much has come. The moment when, lucid at last and free from terror, she asks herself how and why this man is sitting on the edge of her bed. He waits, resigned for the imperious "Out of here!" and that solemn gesture with which women are reported to show one the door in instances like this.

But no. Yolanda puts her head on his chest, pressing against his heart.

Astonished, Juan Manuel does not move. Oh, that delicate temple and the smell of flowering honeysuckle coming from those locks of hair pressed against his lips! He remains motionless for a long time. Motionless, tender, full of wonder—as if an unexpected and priceless treasure had fallen into his arms by accident.

Yolanda! His embrace tightens, pressing her to him. But she cries out—a brief, husky, strange cry—and grabs his arms. They struggle, Juan Manuel entangling himself in her thick, sweet-scented hair. He grapples until he is able to seize her by the neck, and then he brutally throws her down on her back.

Gasping, she tosses her head from side to side, weeping as Juan Manuel kisses her mouth and caresses one of her breasts, small and hard like the camellias she cultivates. So many tears. Running silently down her cheeks, so many tears. Falling on

the pillow like hot watery pearls, dropping into the hollow of his hand still gripping her neck.

Ashamed, his passion ebbing, Juan Manuel relaxes his embrace.

"Do you hate me, Yolanda?"

She is silent, inert.

"Shall I stay?"

Closing her eyes, she whispers: "No, please go."

The wooden floorboards creak as he crosses to the lamp and goes to the door, leaving Yolanda submerged in shadow.

·

On the fourth day, a fine mist shrouds the pampa in a white cottony silence that muffles and shortens the sound of the hunters' guns out on the islands and blinds the frightened storks planing in to seek sanctuary on the lake.

And Yolanda—what is she doing? Juan Manuel wonders. What is she doing while he drags his mud-heavy boots through the reeds, killing birds without reason or passion? Maybe she is in the orchard looking for the last strawberries, or pulling up the first radishes: *One must grasp the leaves tight and take them with a single pull, tearing them out of the dark earth like tiny red hearts.* Or it may be that she is in the house, standing on a stool by an open cupboard, the maid handing her a stack of freshly ironed sheets which she will carefully arrange in even piles. And if she were waiting at the window for his return? Anything is possible with a woman like Yolanda,

such a strange woman, one who resembles a . . . But he checks himself, afraid of hurting her in his thoughts.

.

Twilight again. The hunter gazes across the shadowy pampa, trying to locate the hill and the house. A distant light blinks on amid the fog, pointing the way like a miniature lighthouse.

He drags his boat up the bank and starts across the grassland toward the light. On the way he puts to flight a few head of grazing cattle, their hair twisted into curls by the damp breath of the fog. He leaps barbed-wire fences, the fog clinging to the points like fleece. He sidesteps the thick clumps of thistle that glisten silvery and phosphorescent in the darkness.

Reaching the gate, he crosses the park and goes past the camellias in the garden to a certain window, where he wipes the pane free of fog and then stands transfixed as before his eyes a fairy tale unfolds.

Yolanda is standing naked in the bathroom, absorbed in the contemplation of her right shoulder.

Her right shoulder—on which something light and flexible looms, drooping down to cover a small portion of her back. A wing, or rather, the beginning of a wing. Or more exactly, the stump of a wing. A small atrophied member which she now strokes carefully, as if dreading the touch.

The rest of her body is exactly as he had imagined: slender, proud, and white.

A hallucination, Juan Manuel thinks to himself as he drives crazily, his hands shaking on the steering wheel, along the highway. The long walk, the fog, the weariness, and this state of anxiety I've been living in for the last few days have all combined to make me see what does not exist. Should I go back? But how would I explain my abrupt departure? Don't think about it until you get to Buenos Aires. That's the best thing to do.

By the time he reaches the suburbs of the city, a fine powdery mist coats the windshield. The windshield wipers click like nickel swords, tic-tac, tic-tac, back and forth with a regularity as implacable as his anguish.

He crosses Buenos Aires, dark and deserted in the light shower which bursts into heavy rain as he opens the gate and starts up the walk to his house.

"What's the matter?" his mother asks. "Why have you come back at this hour?"

"My son?"

"Sleeping. It's eleven o'clock, Juan Manuel."

"I want to see him. Good night, Mother."

The old woman shrugs her shoulders and pads off to her room wrapped in a long robe. No, she will never grow accustomed to her son's whims. He is very bright, a fine lawyer; but she would have preferred him less talented and more conventional, like everyone else's sons.

Juan Manuel goes into his son's bedroom and turns on the light. Curled up next to the wall, his head covered by the sheets, the boy resembles a ball of

white twine. Uncovering him, Juan Manuel thinks: He sleeps like an untamed little animal. In spite of the fact that he is nine years old, and notwithstanding his meticulous grandmother.

"Billy, wake up."

The boy sits up in bed, blinks his eyes, and grants his father a sleepy smile.

"I brought you a gift, Billy."

The boy stretches out his hand. Searching through his pockets, Juan Manuel takes out the handkerchief tied into a pouch and hands it to his son. Billy unties the knots and spreads the handkerchief open. Finding nothing, he looks up at his father with a trusting expression, waiting for an explanation.

"It was a kind of flower, Billy—a magnificent jellyfish, I swear. I fished it from the lake for you . . . and it has disappeared . . ."

The boy thinks for a moment and then cries triumphantly: "No, Papa, it didn't disappear; it *melted*. Because jellyfish are made out of water, just water. I learned it in the geography book you gave me."

Outside, the rain lashes the great leaves of the palm tree in the corner of their garden, its shiny-as-patent-leather branches thrashing against the walls.

"You're right, Billy. It melted."

"But . . . jellyfish live in the sea, Papa. How did they get to the lakes?"

"I don't know, son," says Juan Manuel, suddenly tired of the conversation, his mind whirling.

Maybe I should telephone Yolanda, he thinks. Everything might seem less vague, less dreadful if I

could hear her voice—which, like all other voices under similar circumstances, would simply sound distant, a bit surprised by an unexpected call.

He covers Billy and arranges the pillows. Then he goes back down the solemn staircase in that huge house, so cold and ugly in the rain and lightning. The telephone hangs in the hall—another of his mother's inspirations. As he unhooks the small tube-like receiver, a flash of lightning illuminates the front windows from top to bottom. He asks the operator for a number, and while he waits, the deafening thunderclap rolls over the sleeping city like a train roaring through his living room.

And my call, he thinks, now races through the wires under the rain. Now it is passing through Rivadavia with its line of darkened streetlights, and now it is zooming by the suburbs with their muddy flooding pathways, taking now to the freeway and flying along that straight and lonely road until, by now surely, it reaches the vast pampa with its occasional small villages, going like a bullet now across provincial cities where the asphalt glistens like water under the moonlight, and now perhaps shooting out into open country, alone in the rain again, hurtling past a closed railway station, and then dashing across the pasture to the hill, along the poplar-lined drive to dive into the house. And now it rings insistently, echoing and reechoing in the large deserted drawing room, where the wooden floors creak and the roof leaks in one corner.

The ringing resounds for a long time, vibrating

hoarsely in Juan Manuel's ear, echoing sharply in the empty drawing room while he waits anxiously. Then someone suddenly lifts the receiver at the other end. But before the voice can say a word, Juan Manuel slams the receiver onto its hook.

Thinking: If I had said, "I can't go through with it, Yolanda. I've thought it out, believe me. It just isn't possible." If I had at least confirmed my doubts about that horror. But I'm afraid to know the truth.

He climbs the staircase slowly.

There was something more cruel, more punishing than death, after all. And he had believed that death was the final mystery, the ultimate suffering!

Death—that blind alley!

While he grew older, Elsa would remain eternally young, preserved forever at age thirty-three as on the day she departed from this life. And the day would come when Billy would be older than his mother, when he would know more of the world than she.

Think of it: Elsa's hands become dust, yet her very gestures perpetuated in her letters, in the sweater she knitted for him; and those luminous irises of her now empty eyes still shining with life in her photographs . . . Elsa erased, fixed in the earth but yet living in their memory and still part of their everyday life as though her spirit kept growing and could react even to things she once ignored.

Nevertheless, Juan Manuel now knows that there is a condition far more cruel and incomprehensible than any of death's little corollaries, for he has perceived a new mystery: a suffering consisting of amazement and fear.

The light from Billy's bedroom throws a shaft into the dark corridor, inviting him to enter once more in hope of finding his son still awake. But Billy is asleep, and so Juan Manuel looks around the room for something to distract himself and thereby ease his anguish. He goes to Billy's desk and turns the pages of the new geography book. *History of the Earth . . . The Sidereal Phase of the Earth . . . Life in the Paleozoic Era . . .*

And then he reads: *How beautiful must this silent landscape have been in which giant lycopodiums and equisetums raised themselves to such a height, and where mammoth ferns swayed like trees in the humid air . . .*

What landscape is this? he wonders. I cannot have seen it before, surely. Why, then, does it seem so familiar? He turns the page, reading at random: *. . . In any case, it is during the Carboniferous Period when swarms of flying insects appear over the now arborescent regions. During the Late Carboniferous there were insects which possessed three pairs of wings. The most remarkable insects of this Period were very large, similar in shape to our present-day dragonflies but much bigger, having a wingspan of sixty-five centimeters . . .*

Yolanda's dreams, he realizes. The sweet and terrible secret of her shoulder. Perhaps this was where the explanation of the mystery lay.

But Juan Manuel feels incapable of soaring into the intricate galleries of Nature in order to arrive at the mystery's origin. He fears losing his way in that wild world with its disorderly and poorly mapped

pathways, strewn with an unsystematic confusion of clues; fears falling into some dark abyss that no amount of logic will lead him out of. And abandoning Yolanda once more, he closes the book, turns off the light, and leaves the room.